BLOOD ON THE BRAZOS

Book Two in the Series
Trails of Blood and Wine

BLOOD ON THE BRAZOS

Book Two in the Series

Trails of Blood and Wine

PAUL AND MERRILL BONARRIGO

Blood on the Brazos
Book Two in the Series
Trails of Blood and Wine

Publisher: Merbon
4401 Old Reliance Road
Bryan, Texas 77808
979-820-1238

TheVineyardDistrict.com/story/
@mer-bon
@TheVineyardDistrict

Copyeditor: Lynette M. Smith
Cover Design: Abby Parker

Soft Cover ISBN 978-1-7361770-2-0
eBook ISBN: 978-1-7361770-4-4

To Paul and Karen Bonarrigo,

To our grandchildren Paul Anthony and Sophia Marie
Bonarrigo, the next generation of Texas wine pioneers,

and

To Don and Monie Smith, the ultimate encouragers.

We love you all so much! May the Lord forever bless you
and guide your paths.

*"I am the vine; you are the branches. If you remain in
me and I in you, you will bear much fruit; apart
from me you can do nothing."*

John 15:5

This book celebrates the grape grower and winemaker pioneers in the Gulf Coast of Texas and Brazos Bottom.

To the Niederauers who came before us and to those who joined us on our journey, including—the Watsons, the Rice's, the Cottles, and to Ron Perry, George Ray McEachern, Ed and Pat Hiler, Justin Scheiner, Andreea Botezatu, Amit Dhingra, Fran Pontasch Hensz, Michael Cook, Jim Kamas, Chancellor John Sharp, and Fritz Westover, as well as so many more, you are our lionhearted brothers and sisters of the vine. We appreciate your friendship and loyalty.

In *Curse of Estacado*, we left Trevor Talan in the High Plains. He had just learned that he would be joining the faculty at Texas A&M University, where he would be reunited with his friend John Ferris and mentor Dr. George Ray McEachern.

Chapter 1

My drive from Lubbock filled me with sadness and excitement. I was sad to leave my faculty position at Texas Tech and my parents in Oklahoma, but I was excited to be headed towards a new adventure. The Lord was providing the secret desires of my heart to join the staff at Texas A&M University in College Station. On the way, I drove south off the Caprock. In the rear-view mirror, I could see a fifteen-hundred-foot drop off the flat plateau onto prehistoric-looking land ridges that reminded me of the back of a dinosaur. The sagebrush along the way were as big as my car.

The wind was blowing sixty miles per hour. Dust devils swirled on either side of the road. It looked like an old John Wayne western. I expected to see cattle rustlers and wild mustangs racing across the horizon.

Along the way I drove through Texas wine country in Brownfield. Surrounded by lush vineyards on both sides of the road, it was hard to believe that some of the best wines made in America came from grapes grown in this high desert.

The road led me through the sandy land of Seminole and Andrews, through the oil fields of Midland and Odessa, and then on to the beach-like sand dunes of Monahan. Finally, I stopped in Fort Stockton, where I was surprised to find that St. Genevieve Winery had permanently closed. The roof was demolished, and parts of the walls removed. All of the tanks and grape processing equipment were gone. It was another example of the harsh reality of an industry that rewards few and gobbles up many.

Fort Stockton is one of my favorite cities. The people there are so kind to our United States military. Red, white, and blue can be seen everywhere. God Bless America is not just celebrated on the Fourth of July. It felt like home in Oklahoma with my dad at the military base there.

After leaving Fort Stockton, I drove through Ozona, Sonora, and Junction. It was of particular interest to me as I was making my way to Texas A&M University. The "Junction Boys" were famous. Texas A&M football coach Bear Bryant held the team's 1954 pre-season ten-day workout in Junction, Texas. His workouts were legendary. One hundred and fifteen players were subjected to grueling practices in the Texas summer heat and in the midst of a drought. After ten days, only thirty players remained. The story has become part of Texas A&M lore. A movie was made about the story of the "Junction Boys."

The Texas Hill Country wine region reminded me of visiting Tuscany. The rolling hills, breathtaking vistas that appear around every bend, and the many vineyards along the way made me even more excited about my new job adventure at Texas A&M. Plus, rumor had it that Texas A&M, the University of Texas, and Texas Tech were joint venturing to promote Texas wine. It was exciting to be part of a new era of cooperation!

In College Station, I met Dr. George Ray McEachern at the Dixie Chicken. The Dixie Chicken is an Aggie institution known for billiards and beer. What a fitting place to meet a Texas wine pioneer. When I arrived, Dr. McEachern was there to greet me.

"Hello Dr. McEachern. It is such a pleasure to be with you again and to join the faculty at Texas A&M University. It's an honor to take your place on the faculty. Yours will be hard shoes to fill. I hope now that you'll be retiring, we'll have many opportunities for you to tell me more about Texas wine history.

George Ray chuckled. "That would take years. I know where all the bodies are buried."

I told him I had already begun digging up some of those bodies.

He replied, "Thank you, Trevor. It's a pleasure to see you again and to welcome you to the Aggie family. I hope you have a lot of maroon and white clothing!

"I plan to do some traveling, but I want you to meet Dr. Gail Johnson, who has worked with me for many years. She can share much of the Texas wine history, especially the history of the Brazos River and East Texas.

"Gail, this is Trevor Talan," he said. "He's the viticulture professor joining us that I told you about. His passion is grape and wine history, with a nose for forensics."

"Yes, Trevor, I read about you in the book, *The Curse of Estacado*," She replied as she shook my hand. "I enjoyed reading it. Little did I know the Comanche curse could have such a profound impact on grape growing on the High Plains. You know, there are many mysteries about the grape and wine industry, and I appreciated your thorough detective work.

"What I hear about the high plains industry is that it continues to be a revolving door of players. Winemakers, production staff, and vineyard consultants are hired and fired daily. I hope this does not result in mysterious events and another round of bankruptcies and deaths. There is a lot of money at stake. I hope we can't blame the Comanches this time."

"Thank you, Dr. Johnson. I enjoyed the discovery process and was especially satisfied to learn about my Comanche heritage. So, tell me about your heritage. What is your educational experience in horticulture?"

"Please call me Gail, Trevor. Why don't we grab a beer, and I'll tell you all about it." On the way to the bar, she shared that her introduction to horticulture began at Cornell University for her Bachelor of Science and master's degrees. Once we sat down, she continued, "I went to Texas A&M University for my Ph.D. specializing in fruit production. Dr. McEachern was my Ph.D. advisor. As the grape industry grew, I began assisting growers and educating myself on wines made from the grapes we could grow."

Dr. Johnson was an attractive white-haired woman with a commanding presence. She shared with me that she had never married, and in her spare time, she raised Yorkshire terriers. One of her dogs won the Westminster Kennel Club Dog Show in New York. She had dedicated her entire life to her passions for horticulture and terriers.

"I look forward to hearing about your experiences, Gail. The Grand Commander of the Houston Chapter of the Knights of the Vine, Buddy Hagner, has asked me to write about the history of Texas wine, and I planned to get right into my research before the fall semester. Your help will be invaluable. Buddy told me to meet an Italian American, Luigi Cannoli of the *Brenham Daily News*. Evidently, Luigi has done extensive research on Texas wine history as well."

"It sounds like you have many valuable resources, Trevor. Do you have time for me to tell you what I know about Brazos Bottom Texas wine history?"

Excitedly, I said, "I have all the time in the world."

Chapter 2

"In 1831," Dr. Johnson explained, "Frederick Ernst received a grant and brought a large group of German immigrants to Austin County, Texas. The settlement was called Adelsverein. They were the first group to plant grapes in Austin County. Then, in 1844, three shiploads of Germans settled what they called New Braunfels and Fredericksburg in central Texas. They planted grapes too.

"In 1880 Count Giuseppe Telfener of Sicily and William Palmer, a wealthy businessman from New York, embarked on a plan to build a railroad from Mexico to New York. Count Telfener had just completed a three hundred fifty-mile line in Argentina. The state of Texas incentivized the project by offering sixteen sections of land for every completed mile of track. Telfener imported one thousand two hundred Italian laborers from northern Italy in the region of Lombardy. They began construction of the railroad simultaneously in Richmond, Texas, and Brownsville, Texas. They worked toward each other hoping to meet in Victoria, Texas.

"Macaroni was the most common meal of the workers, hence the name "Macaroni Railroad". The crew worked for six months. Many laborers became sick, and half the crew died or quit.

"In July of 1882, construction was halted, and the state of Texas repealed all of the land grants. Ninety-one miles of track were laid at a cost of two million dollars. Count Telfener operated the railroad from 1882 until 1884 when he sold the railroad to John Mackey, who then sold the railroad to Southern Pacific Railroad in 1885. Count Telfener had planned to bring an additional five thousand Italians, but when construction was halted, that plan was never realized. After the project was cancelled and the railroad was sold, Count Telfener and his family returned to Rome, Italy. Many of the workers that survived the construction of the Macaroni Railroad settled in Central Texas.

Henri Castro brought Alsatians and Italians from Torino, Italy, to Castroville. The Macaroni Railroad Line brought the Qualia family to Del Rio. Their Val Verde Winery is the oldest winery in Texas. All these cultures brought grape growing and winemaking traditions from their home countries."

I told her that I remembered reading about the Qualia family when I was doing the research for *The Curse of Estacado*. They are a legend in the Texas wine industry. They planted Lenoir, Champanel, and Herbermont grapes. The Qualia family named their winery Val Verde, which means "Green Valley." Val Verde winery survived prohibition by selling sacramental wine to the Catholic church.

She asked, "Are you familiar with T. V. Munson?" I smiled and said, "Sure. Everyone in the Texas wine industry knows he's the Texas-French connection in wine. He received the Legion of Honor Award from France because he saved the French grape industry by planting Texas rootstock in French vineyards and grafting European grapes on top to overcome phylloxera."

"Not only did he save the industry," reflected Gail, "he brought focus to the many rootstocks that are indigenous to

Texas. Texas has eighteen of the twenty-seven known rootstocks.

"He realized from early Texas immigrants that, when they planted European grapevines near native grapevines, the European grapevines died within six years. We later discovered that they were dying of Anaheim Disease, also known as Pierce's Disease, but American varieties did not get the disease. It is not native to the United States but was introduced into the USA from Central America.

"Pierce's Disease is a deadly grape disease that was first discovered by Dr. Pierce, a University of California professor. In 1884, while investigating the decline of vineyards in Anaheim, California, he found that a sharpshooter insect injects a bacterium into the grapevine, causing it to clog water-conducting vessels within the plants, resulting in death. The glassy winged sharpshooter is a small hopping, and sometimes flying, half-inch-size insect with bulging yellow eyes and transparent wings."

It sounded like something from a sci-fi movie. It was hard to imagine something so small could kill grapevines. Pierce's Disease did not exist in the High Plains, so I was unfamiliar with this problem.

"My preliminary research revealed that by the 1930's, there were five winery families in the Brenham, Texas, area—the Bonders, the Kistys, the Niders, the Metocks, and the Galles'," I said. They produced 62,000 gallons of wine, and the locals say the five families were very competitive."

Gail said, "That is my understanding as well, Trevor, and there were family intermarriages. One of the Bonder family daughters married Phillip Kisty's oldest son, Ben, who is a strapping, God-fearing young man. The two wineries combined to make the BonderKisty Winery. Ben's brother Louis, a tall, thin, long-faced young man who worked at the winery, oversaw their construction projects. BonderKisty became the largest winery in the region.

"The Nider family had two daughters, and their father, Bob, is reputed to be one of Texas' finest winemakers—or at least that's what he says he is. He's successful at making Germanic style wines. The family originated from Koblenz in the Rhine Valley and came to Brenham after World War I. Many German families immigrated to Texas to avoid serving in the German Army.

"The Metock family story you can learn from an old-time grape grower named Charlie Gee. He's been around for many years and lives near Brenham in the Brazos Bottom.

"The Galle family was from Palermo, Sicily. There was a suspicion that the family was from a Mafia family in the old country and had to move to America. The Galle family consisted of two boys and two girls. The boys worked in the winery; Peter made the wine, and Tony worked the bottling line. The two girls, Rose and Violet, worked in the thirty-acre vineyard. The parents, Alfonse and Ester, were devoted to the family business. The two sons had horrible reputations with gambling and drinking. Peter was known to have card tables set up for gambling in his home. He also liked to bet on the horse tracks of Kentucky. Tony was very mechanical. He could take the bottling line apart with his eyes closed. The two girls were very dedicated to their parents.

"Rose and Violet rarely dated. Rose attended college and studied grape growing at U. C. Davis in California. Violet was the older of the two and learned her vineyard skills on the job. Their vineyard was said to be the most beautiful in Texas. It looked like a garden."

Gail continued, "Rose was not a good tractor driver. Rose was not even a good car driver. She once filled up with gas and drove off with the gas hose still left in the gas tank. She almost blew up the gas station. She was so short that, when she drove, she could barely see over the steering wheel. Violet loved to drive the spray rig but flunked the state test three times and had poor math skills. When you spray, you need basic math and knowledge of chemicals. Rose insisted on doing the spraying because of Violet's shortcomings. Violet feared that Rose would injure herself and run over the grapevines. They were quite a pair."

Chapter 3

I asked Gail about growing conditions in the Brazos Valley.

She responded, "Growing grapes in the Brazos Bottom is tough. Rain during harvest is always a threat. Spring freezes and winter kill are common. Every region of the world has its challenges. But the wines made from Brazos Bottom grapes are well received in international competitions."

I asked her what made the Brazos Bottom so good for wine.

She answered, "The soil of the Bottom is sandy loam created by the confluence of two of Texas's great rivers—the mighty Brazos and the Navasota. The Brazos River is 1,280 miles long, beginning at the head of Blackwater Draw in New Mexico and ending at the Gulf of Mexico. The soil is filled with nutrients from upstream and is some of the best soil in Texas. The Brazos River is the most historic river in Texas. It was navigable and influential due to its proximity to "Washington on the Brazos," the Texas Republic's Capital and the site of the first convention of Texas lawmakers.

"The Navasota River is 125 miles long, beginning near Mount Calm, Texas, and flowing south into the Brazos River. The Brazos and the Navasota are not only rivers that produced some of the most fertile land in the United States. The climate of the Brazos Bottom is like Bordeaux. It's mild and temperate climate is influenced by the Gulf of Mexico, as the Bordeaux climate is influenced by the Atlantic.

"When the French Explorer LaSalle helped settle the region, he encouraged the planting of grapes in the Brazos Bottom. There is a statue of him in Navasota. Many immigrants have come to the Brazos Bottom and have found fertile soil and agricultural riches. Many lives have been enhanced and lost over these fertile soils so rich in history."

"What stands out in the grapes that is different?" I asked.

She shared, "The two primary grapes are Blanc du Bois—a white grape, and Lenoir—a dark red teinturier grape which means it free-runs red juice instead of light pink juice. There are not many teinturier grape varieties.

"The Blanc du Bois grape was created in 1968 by a Texan, John Mortensen, at the University of Florida's Central Florida Research and Educational Center. Mortensen created the variety by crossing vinifera with golden muscat and native Florida varieties. It is two thirds European vinifera with the rest being from American varietals. The grape was released in 1987 and produces wines with an aroma of lemon zest, peach, and mandarin orange. They have successfully produced dry, sweet, and sparkling wine styles from this grape, which is the most planted white variety in Texas.

"The Lenoir grape has a mysterious history, though it has been documented to have been grown on the island of Madeira and used in Madeira wines during the time of Benjamin Franklin and the American Revolution. Records reveal the grape originated in South Carolina around 1830 and was later hybridized in Montpelier, France. It is a naturally occurring hybrid that is 69 percent European vinifera Cabernet Franc. The rest of the parentage is American.

"In the 1800s, Lenoir journeyed to Madeira. Lenoir has many names. Other names include Jack, Blue French, Chavez, and Jacquez. The interesting thing about this grape is that it reaches a high sugar content and makes a great Port wine. One winery makes Port style wine without the addition of high-proof spirits. It is naturally fermented using a unique technique called *sequential inoculation*, which was developed by Paul Vincent Bonarrigo, who was one of the founders of Messina Hof Winery and a winemaker for many years."

"I have never heard of sequential inoculation," I said. "What is it?"

She smiled. "Sequential inoculation requires an initial introduction of yeast to the grapes. Then, one week later, a sequential inoculation of yeast is followed by three additional yeast additions one week apart. This continues until the alcohol level reaches 18.5 percent. There is no need to add brandy to reach the required alcohol level. The resulting wine is smoother and ready to drink earlier. Some of the judges remarked that this three-year-old Port resembled a twenty-year-old Portuguese Ruby Port."

There was so much more to learn about Dr. Johnson. She traveled to Burgundy and brought students and Texas winemakers to learn from French winemakers. She shared stories of how they studied in the mornings at the University of Dijon, a sister university to TAMU, and then toured Burgundy Chateaux in the afternoons where they met with the winemakers of each Chateau.

She was pleased to say, "Their experience was fantastic. I believe that their experiences changed the Texas industry.

They discovered that terroir is particularly important. The same grapes, Chardonnay and Pinot Noir, can be planted on varying sites and have completely different flavor profiles. In Burgundy, there were differences in soil type and elevation, just as is true in the Brazos Bottom.

"In the Brazos Bottom, elevations vary from 20 to 280 feet, and soil types vary from sandy loam to clay loam. One important example is Lenoir. It can have a cherry aroma when grown in the lower bottom on sandy loam, but it develops a deep dark chocolate flavor when it is grown at a higher elevation in heavier clay soil."

Dr. Johnson was the first to write about the importance of terroir in the Brazos Bottom. Most people thought the entire Brazos Bottom was one terroir until she pointed out the dramatic differences in soil types and its impact on Lenoir. People did not appreciate the difference initially.

"My latest research has proved that Blanc du Bois has a vastly different aroma as well. When planted in sandy loam, it has aromas of citrus reminiscent of New Zealand Sauvignon Blanc. When planted in clay loam at higher elevations, the aroma is reminiscent of French Sancerre Sauvignon Blanc."

Her work has made the discussion of terroir much more meaningful to the wineries of the Brazos Bottom.

We spoke for two hours. She encouraged me to call Luigi and to share what I learned. I called Luigi at once and set up a meeting for lunch at Royer's Roundtop Café.

I decided to call my dear friend John Ferris. John and I did all of the research on *The Curse of Estacado*, and he was instrumental in helping me get the job at Texas A&M University. I had not seen him since I arrived, so I invited him to join us at the Round Top Café, and he eagerly accepted. Royer's Round Top Café is an iconic Texas Bistro. Bud and Karen Royer along with their four children moved to Round Top and bought the café' in 1987.

It was a leap of faith and truly a family affair. They worked side by side in the restaurant and in the marketing. It was such an inspiring story, I wanted to see for myself.

Bud is known as "The Pieman." The café is a tiny forty-seat restaurant that has made a significant impact on Texas cuisine and pie making. Round Top's population is ninety-three people, and yet it is known as one of American's largest antique markets.

Chapter 4

Royer's was on my bucket list, and I looked forward to experiencing it in person. So many people told me about the great food and Royer family. The pies were shipped all over the world. American Presidents served his pies in the White House. Bud is a culinary legend in Texas, and his children have continued the business legacy.

The drive from College Station to Round Top is one of the prettiest drives in the entire state of Texas. As John and I drove through Gay Hill, we could see fields of colorful wildflowers and the backdrop of Lake Somerville in the distance.

When we arrived in Round Top, I saw a man sitting on the porch, waiting. He was iconic looking, with his long white beard, and with his jovial personality greeted John and me with a strong handshake. He introduced himself as Bud. Then a fourth man approached the three of us.

"Howdy, I am Luigi Cannoli. Nice to meet you all. Thank you for coming."

Bud greeted him first and then introduced John and me.

As we entered the café, I was mesmerized by the walls and ceilings covered with memorabilia and photos. The room looked like a three-dimensional scrapbook of history. We sat near the pie safe, which was filled with the most delicious looking and smelling pies.

I was focused on which one I should try, when Luigi spoke. "I have been assigned to research the story of Texas grape growing in East Texas. My editor, Bubba Biggie, of the

Brenham Daily News, assigned me to tell the story of how Brenham influenced the history of Texas wine. He told me that the Brazos Bottom was one of the first regions in Texas to develop a grape community.

"As the Brenham to Independence area was settled, Independence, Texas, was founded by Sam Houston and became associated with Baylor University. Strongly Baptist, they did not encourage winemaking or drinking alcohol.

"The German, French and Italian settlers brought traditions of growing grapes, grain, and making wine and beer."

I asked Luigi to tell us more about his background.

Luigi started talking. "I grew up in Little Italy of the Bronx, New York. Both of my parents were born in Sicily. Both came to America when they were teenagers. I saw my first tree when I was twelve. My neighborhood was a concrete canyon. Not even one blade of grass grew there. I went to elementary school at P.S. 32, where I learned how to swim. Mr. Silverman was my swim teacher."

I told Luigi that I learned to swim in a lake in Lawton, Oklahoma, with the cows looking at me.

Luigi laughed. "In the city, most of our play was on the street. My mom would watch me from the fourth-floor window. On weekends, my dad would take me to the baseball fields. Back then, if you took a match book and a quarter, you could sit in the bleachers at Yankee Stadium. The Yankees were fantastic during those years. My childhood heroes were Mickey Mantle, Roger Maris, and Yogi Berra."

I was fascinated by his storytelling. His upbringing was much different than this Oklahoma guy.

He continued, "My family moved to Cresskill, New Jersey, when I was in fifth grade. I attended Tenafly High School. My dad said, 'I am proud of you, and I will help you pay for college.' He then gave me a $5 bill and said that he would give me $5 every month, as long as I kept my grades up. I was shocked. College was much more expensive than $60/year. Thank goodness I went to college on a scholarship, and I worked for the Columbia student newspaper. Life at Columbia was quite different than my Italian American upbringing in the Bronx. Most of my Columbia classmates were from very wealthy families.

"After my degree in journalism from Columbia, I could not find a journalist's job in New York. I started looking elsewhere and found a job listing for the *Brenham Daily News* newspaper in Brenham, Texas. I attended Brenham Elementary school in New Jersey. Do you believe in destiny? This must have been an omen from God. 'Go West, young man!'"

We laughed, and I nodded my head, recognizing that Luigi and I would make a great team.

"When I flew into Houston, the editor of the *Brenham Daily News* met me at the airport. His name was Bubba Biggie. Great name, because he was at least six-foot-four and weighed 300 pounds. He greeted me with a mouthful of chew and asked me if I wanted some Copenhagen. I told him I thought that was a city in Denmark. He laughed out loud and spit into a Styrofoam cup. I thought chewing tobacco was only for baseball players.

"Bubba told me that he started as a sports reporter. When all of the editor staff quit, he became the editor. He graduated from Brenham High School and had been with the paper for thirty years.

"His family were cotton farmers in the Brazos Bottom. Bubba's great-grandfather worked for the Folder family doing accounting services. After over thirty years of service, Mr. Folder deeded Bubba's great-grandfather fifty acres to raise cotton. When Bubba's great-grandfather passed, he left the land to Bubba's grandfather; and when he passed, Bubba's dad owned the farm. Bubba wanted to do something different, so after high school he got a job first as a copy boy at the newspaper, and then as a sports reporter.

"Bubba was married to his high school sweetheart, Matilda, and they had six children ranging in age from six to thirty. Bubba seemed like a wonderful man. Everywhere you go in Brenham, people say Bubba is a hero. Twenty years ago, a Brenham football player passed out on the field. The trainers all ran out onto the field. The player's lifeless body lay on the fifty-yard line. No one seemed to know what to do. Bubba was covering the game for the paper and became alarmed at the incident. He ran out onto the field and immediately began CPR. He saved that player's life.

"After that Bubba got to know all of the coaches and all of the players. He traveled with the team and was trusted by the coaches and the families of the players. Bubba always spoke kindly of the coaches and the teams. When they lost, Bubba would always see the positive side of the story and share it in the newspaper. Bubba is a true local hero, and everyone loves him.

"Bubba was curious about my New York heritage and told me he wanted to visit New York someday. Bubba told me he thought I would be the first New Yorker to ever work at the *Brenham News*.

"The newspaper put me up at the Howard Johnson hotel, and Bubba was to pick me up the next morning to take me to Brenham. I was hungry, so went to eat at a local diner. There were foods that I had never heard of, so I tried something that sounded interesting. I had my first tamale. The waiter asked me if I had ever had a tamale. I said "sure" so as not to be exposed as a newbie. When the tamale arrived, I started eating it. It was the toughest thing I had ever eaten.

"The waiter came back to my table, stood there, and watched me, and finally broke the awkward chewing, saying, 'I have never seen a person eat the husk.' I swallowed my pride and asked, 'How do you eat a tamale'?

"The waiter smiled and said, 'Remove the husk and eat what is inside. You are not from here, are you?'

"I answered, 'No, I am from New York, and I just graduated from Columbia University.'

"The waiter tried to chat. 'I've heard of that school. Is it in South America?' I soon realized my Ivy League education had little value in Texas."

John Ferris laughed and shared that he had the same tamale experience when he moved to Texas. "I went to the Mama Maria Cantina in San Antonio while attending an A&M basketball game. I ordered tamales on the recommendation of another student. He never said a word as he watched me struggle with chewing the fibrous husk. After a few minutes of watching me chew, he started laughing out loud. Then he told me I was not supposed to eat it. Once I learned how to eat them properly, I really enjoyed them." Luigi agreed.

Luigi continued his story. "Then, I noticed at the next table a man eating what I thought was a veal cutlet with a strange white gravy all over it. I asked the waiter what that was. He said it was chicken fried steak.

"When I commented that it must be a chicken breast pounded into a cutlet, the waiter looked shocked and said there is no chicken. It is steak!

"Wow, that was a chicken dish without chicken. He said the gravy was white flour and milk. What strange food!"

John laughed again and went on to share with Luigi how He and I had met in Oklahoma at a conference and continued to work together on *The Curse of Estacado* project. He joked, "It's being considered by Martin Scorsese as a movie adapted from our book."

Chapter 5

While we were talking, Luigi received a phone call from Bubba Biggie. Luigi hung up and said to me, "Are you up for your first Brazos Bottom adventure? Bubba gave us a lead."

"Yes, let's go." John left us to our investigation, and Luigi drove me to the crash scene. There was an overturned tractor. A farm worker told us that the victim was taken to the hospital. Luigi asked, "Who was the victim?" The worker replied, "Rose Galle".

I recognized that name from my conversation with Dr. Johnson. Rose was the daughter of Alphonse and Ester Galle.

Luigi looked at me and said, "This is major! I wonder if their past has caught up with them?" We went to the hospital to see if we could talk with Rose. She looked like a mummy, all wrapped up in the hospital bed. Luigi introduced us and asked if she could tell us what happened.

She spoke slowly. "It was so bright and calm this morning. I was ready to cultivate the vineyard. It was the first cultivation of the season. I checked the tractor and filled it with gas. It was clean and ready to go. I drove the tractor through a steep slope in the vineyard. When I made the turn at the end of a row, I must have been driving too fast. The tractor listed to the left. I tried to correct my mistake, but it was too late. The tractor turned over and I was trapped under it when I was thrown out of the cab." She stopped talking and stared at her hands for a moment. Then looking up at us she asked, "Is my dad angry?"

Luigi and I looked at each other and said, "Hope you get better soon.' Then we went back to the scene and looked at the tractor. Luigi noticed the left front tire was almost flat. So, when Rose tried to turn, the tire caused her to flip the tractor. I looked at Luigi and asked how the tire could become so flat so quickly without her noticing.

Luigi suggested, "Poor maintenance? Did someone deliberately deflate the tire? If so, who? Why?"

We went to see Rose's parents. Her father seemed both sad and angry. Luigi asked him about tire maintenance.

He responded, "Rose was very careful about maintaining the tractor. The tractor was her baby. She loved that tractor and enjoyed working on it as much as riding in it. She cared for it like her car."

Luigi asked if we could see the maintenance log. Alphonse was happy to help. All of the tire pressures recorded looked normal. We thanked the parents and returned to the tractor. By now the police were there. They found her phone on the ground. She must have lost it when she was thrown. Luigi asked the police if we could see the phone. The police told us to meet Sergeant Jeffries the next day at the police station.

Sergeant Jeffries was a military policeman from Winnie, Texas. Luigi told me, "When Jeffries left the service, he brought his new wife to Brenham. They were starting a new life, and he wanted the opportunity to join the Sheriff's department."

He was five-foot-nine, weighed 165 pounds, and was in great physical shape. His physique made me think I really needed to start going to the gym.

Luigi said, "When he was in the service, he met his wife Fatama, who was from Iraq. At first the Brenham community was suspicious of Fatama's intentions. She was from a different culture. She had an accent and barely spoke English. You know, fear of the unknown. Outsiders to Brazos Bottom have difficulty adjusting to such a small, close-knit community. Once Fatama joined the Brazos Bottom Bible Church and Sergeant Jeffries started volunteering at the food bank, the community softened towards them. Now they are accepted in the Brazos Bottom community."

I learned that Sergeant Jeffries was an expert in advanced interrogation techniques. He left the service under a cloud of suspicion as to how aggressive and advanced those interrogation techniques were. When Sergeant Jeffries met Rose, he was very soft and gentle in his approach.

Sergeant Jeffries was curious about what was on the phone. He said, "There are many text messages from a man she is seeing. The messages were to break off her relationship with him. She also had messages from her sister, Violet, who appeared to be worried about the relationship. Violet texted her sister that the '… guy is violent and has a quick temper. Please break it off!' Rose wrote. 'I will meet with the guy to let him down gently and avoid a larger blowup.' The last text was the night before Rose's accident."

When Luigi examined the tractor, he found a nail in the tire. He shook his head and said, "The reason for the low tire was the nail, but it does not make sense that Rose got on the tractor with low tire pressure. She is too particular."

I asked, "How do you think the nail got there? When I looked at the nail, I realized that it wasn't the type of nail used in the vineyard; it's the type used in framing a house with a nail gun."

"This points to Louis, who is a son of Phillip Kisty of the BonderKisty Winery." Luigi warned, "If Louis is responsible, it will make relations between the two winery families go very badly."

Louis was brought in for questioning, and he immediately told Sergeant Jeffries that he thought the accident was caused by Rose's sister.

Louis claimed, "I spoke with Violet the night before the accident, and she told me that she was going to do whatever it took to keep Rose out of the tractor."

I could see that Sergeant Jeffries had a dilemma. He had two primary suspects—Violet and Louis. Just then, he got a call from the lab. They found a piece of cloth from a man's glove stuck in between the nail and the tire.

Sergeant Jeffries confronted Louis. Initially, Louis explained, "Violet was not as sweet as many people thought. Violet was bipolar. She could be extremely sweet, but she could be very moody. She loved her sister, but they had sibling rivalry. Sometimes they dated the same guys."

Sergeant Jeffries talked with Louis for thirty minutes. Then he mentioned to Louis that they had found a piece of cloth that they believed was from a man's glove. Louis's composure changed dramatically. He no longer mentioned Violet. He started to explain how he was busy all day. He became more defensive. Louis could see that the glove cloth would reveal that the DNA would be his. Louis started to cry.

He said, "I just wanted to damage the wheel so she would call me to repair the tire. I never expected her to turn over the tractor."

The sergeant told Louis he was calling his father. In fact, he called the fathers of both families to meet. He told us, "Preventing a war between the wine families is very important."

Louis's father, Phillip Kisty, and Rose's father, Alphonse Galle, came in for the pow-wow. Both fathers heard the news and appeared shocked. Neither knew about the relationship. After sharing their dismay, the men shook hands, but I could feel the animosity in the air. Mr. Galle was not known to forgive and forget. Phillip Kisty agreed to repair the tractor. He was noticeably quiet when the sergeant told him that his son would have to plead guilty and serve three months in the county jail.

Louis had no prior criminal record, so the judge ordered probation. So as long as Louis remained good for the next six months, his record would be cleared. Louis and Rose broke up. They were not good for each other.

Rose started dating the football coach at Brenham High School. Her father introduced them while Louis was in jail. They seemed perfect for each other, and Alphonse Galle loved going to high school football games.

After getting out of jail, Louis started dating a woman in Houston and spent most of his weekends there. He called Rose a few times, but Rose would not answer. Finally, Rose blocked his number. On occasion, Louis dropped by the vineyard to see Rose, but she was not receptive. Finally, Louis got the message that Rose was not interested in his advances. He spent more time in Houston.

Chapter 6

I told Luigi about my conversation with Dr. Johnson and asked him if he had met Charlie Gee. Luigi said he had, and I shared that I would be interested in hearing Charlie's story. Luigi and I made a date to meet up the next evening and begin our collaboration. He wanted me to witness a Friday evening ritual in the Brazos Bottom. I was intrigued.

It was foggy that evening in the Brazos Bottom. Luigi picked me up and took me to the picnic grounds near the church. On the way he prepared me by saying, "All the wine families get together for a night of gambling. It is known that many acres of land have been won and lost at a card table." He said, "Everyone, including the sergeant, knows about the gambling; but after a hard week of agricultural work, it is a good way to blow off steam. Usually, the card games are friendly, but sometimes tempers flare up and farmlands are lost. Crap tables and roulette tables are set up, and donations are collected to help local charities.

"Tonight, will be especially fun because tomorrow is the annual Best of the Bottom wine competition. Wine judges are brought in from all over. They will be here tonight. Two of them are from California, one from France, one from New York, and one from Italy."

I remembered that Dr. Johnson had said several of the wines had won major awards, so I asked Luigi about the awards criteria.

He shared, "All of the wines must be grown and produced from grapes grown in the Brazos Bottom. Fifty wines will be judged—twenty-five white wines and twenty-five red wines. There are bets on the table tonight on who will win.

"Each of the five wine families can submit ten wines—five white wines and five red ones. Each wine is scored individually and then their scores are averaged. The top red and white wine is awarded Best of the Bottom. The top wines' scores are then averaged to award the Top Brazos Bottom Winery. It is a major bragging right for the next twelve months. All the area restaurants support the competition by putting the winning wines on their wine lists, and the Top Brazos Bottom Winery has wine dinners in each of the best Bottom restaurants."

"When do they announce the winners?" I asked.

"It is usually after harvest is over and all the grapes are fermenting. That is when everyone has time to pause for a celebration. It doubles as the end-of-harvest celebration, too."

As we arrived, the country casino was just as Luigi described. We parked, got out of the car, and walked toward the gambling tables. Luigi suddenly started waving to an elderly gentleman sitting near the fire pit. He had white hair and a white beard and looked just like Santa Claus. He was surrounded by young people, and he was telling stories. They were hanging on to his every word.

"Hello, Charlie," said Luigi. "How have you been? Still teaching, I see." Charlie Gee laughed. Luigi introduced me and asked if Charlie minded sharing some of his stories with me. I walked up to him and extended my hand. Charlie's hand was large and rough. I could tell he had worked with grapes for many years.

Charlie nodded, pointed me to a chair, and began to speak with a deep, resonating voice that cracked. Charlie had obviously told these timeless tales of growing grapes in the Brazos Bottom many times.

He began, "On my first visit to these nights of gambling, I watched the head of the Nizzi family lose three hundred acres when he bet on a full house and lost to a straight flush. His wife did not allow him in the house for a month. He slept in his pickup. Thank goodness it was in the spring! Mr. Nizzi gave up gambling after that one. He told his wife he gave away his lowest yielding acreage, and she forgave him and let him back in the house. That was smart on his part because I think he would have stayed in that pickup."

I told him that Dr. Johnson had told me Bob Nider was acclaimed to be the best winemaker. Charlie chuckled.

He paused and then said, "Bob Nider makes good wines. He is a driven man and determined to succeed. He runs his family like a good German soldier.

"His grandfather, Adler, was Prussian and refused the draft in his country, so he emigrated to Texas through Ellis Island. After connecting with other German immigrants, he learned about Brenham and came here as a chocolate maker. He made chocolate for all the wealthy families of the Brenham area. He was a prudent man and saved his money enough to purchase the land where Nider Winery exists. Adler sent his grandson, Bob, to the University of California at Davis to study winemaking.

"Bob came back to Brenham and made the reputation of a great winemaker. His wife, Dolphie, continued the tradition of chocolate candies and desserts. She is famous for her German chocolate cake. It has become our regional recipe.

"Their daughters, Annie and Beulah, help their mother make the desserts. Beulah married Presley, and they have three children—Franz, Frasie, and Flo. Annie married Louis. They have two children, Flory and Martin.

"All of the grandchildren are fantastic students. They are on the dean's list at school. All of them work in the winery cleaning tanks and working in the lab. On harvest days, they help with picking and sorting the grapes. Their father doesn't have to tell them what to do. They just do it."

I was impressed and said so.

Charlie continued. "Beulah's husband, Presley, was a mechanic for a well-known race car driver, A.W. He had toured the world with A.W. When A.W. had a race at the Texas World Speedway in College Station, Presley oversaw A.W.'s pit crew.

Beulah was responsible for catering to the pit crews and met Presley over a croissant. Presley said he had never tasted anything so wonderful. Beulah was smitten. Presley gave up the high life with A.W. and married Beulah.

"Presley repairs equipment in the winery. He can fix anything. He is great friends with the owner of the Brenham Electric Motor Services. Between the two of them, they can fix any motor.

"Annie's husband, Blue, oversees the bottling line. He was working for Tony Wine Equipment out of Fresno as the head mechanic. When the family bought a new bottling line, Blue was sent to set it up. While Blue was setting up the line, he met Annie. She helped Blue settle in. She was young and flirtatious. Blue, of course, was impressed. The setup of the bottling line took twice as long as usual, mostly because Blue paid more attention to Annie than setting up the bottling line.

"Tony called Blue and asked what was going on. Blue said he thought it would be three more days, but he was not coming back to Fresno. Tony asked why. Blue replied, 'I have found a home in Texas, and I am going to marry Annie.'

"Tony was angry at first, but respected true love. Blue left Tony and married Annie. Blue took over the bottling line that he had set up. Before he took over, bottling was a disaster. The machine had not been maintained and was constantly breaking. But ever since Blue took over, the bottling line-has run like a well-oiled machine.

"Annie and Beulah work well together in the vineyard. They took classes in viticulture from Dr. McEachern."

Dr. McEachern! I was elated. "I know Dr. McEachern!" I said, "I'm the one who took Dr. McEachern's position when he retired." Charlie nodded and seemed pleased.

Then he continued, "Bob is a consistent winemaker. He is particularly good with white wines. His favorite wine to make is Blanc Du Bois, which grows well here. He makes it in a German style in stainless steel and finishes it dry. Some of Bob's secrets in making a great Blanc DuBois are that he picks his grapes at two a.m., and he stops picking at daybreak. He lays his grapes on straw mats until noon of the following day. He removes all excess water from the cluster which makes the juice more concentrated with more flavor.

"Bob cold-settles the must for twenty-four hours at 33 degrees Fahrenheit, just above freezing. He cultures his own yeast by scraping yeast off of the berry and picks his grapes by taste and not by a predetermined sugar level. He ferments very slowly at 40 degrees Fahrenheit for eight weeks, pumping the grape solids over the top to give his wine a creamy consistency. After fermentation, he allows the wine to settle and does not filter. Annually, Bob bottles the new vintage on the day before Thanksgiving and usually sells out before Christmas. It is their biggest seller, and he will tell you that he thinks this vintage will be his best."

Charlie concluded, "Time will tell. We will see at the end of harvest."

Chapter 7

I changed the subject because I was fascinated by the German chocolate cake story. "Charlie," I said, "I love chocolate cake, and I wonder where I might get some of that famous German chocolate cake." He referred me to a local bakery but said I could find the recipe in the local *Brenham Cookbook*.

Luigi spoke up, "I have a copy and can share it with you."

German Chocolate Cake

Ingredients for Cake

- 4 ounces German sweet chocolate, broken into small pieces
- 1 cup butter, room temperature
- 2 cups sugar
- 4 large eggs, room temperature
- 1 teaspoon vanilla extract
- 2-1/2 cups cake flour
- 1 teaspoon baking soda
- 1/2 teaspoon salt
- 1 cup buttermilk
- 1 teaspoon ground cloves

Ingredients for Icing

- 1-1/2 cups sugar
- 1-1/2 cups evaporated milk
- 3/4 cup butter
- 6 large egg yolks, room temperature, beaten
- 2 cups sweetened shredded coconut
- 2 cups chopped pecans
- 1-1/2 teaspoons vanilla extract

Directions for Cake

1. Preheat oven to 350 degrees F.

2. Grease three 9-inch round baking pans with quick release cake pan goop. Set aside.

3. Melt chocolate in a double boiler over low heat. Set aside.

4. In a large bowl, cream butter, and sugar until light and fluffy, 5–7 minutes. Beat in 4 eggs, 1 at a time, until smooth. Blend in melted chocolate and vanilla.

5. Sift together flour, baking soda, salt, and cloves.

6. Add to the creamed mixture alternately with buttermilk, beating well after each addition.

7. Pour batter into prepared pans. Bake 24–28 minutes or until a toothpick inserted in center comes out clean.

8. Cool 5 minutes before removing from pans to wire racks to cool completely.

Directions for Icing

1. In small saucepan, heat sugar, milk, butter, and egg yolks over medium-low heat until mixture is thickened and golden brown, stirring constantly for about 15 minutes. When it is thick like pudding and bubbling, remove from heat.

2. Stir in coconut, pecans, and vanilla. Cool until thick enough to spread.

3. Spread a third of the frosting over each cake layer and stack the layers.

Luigi said, "Charlie Gee was from Santa Rosa California. He worked in all the famous vineyards of Napa and Sonoma. He was the ultimate vineyard manager. He planted vineyards for all the great wineries."

"After twenty years in Napa," Charlie said, "I met the love of my life, Maria. She was from the Brazos Bottom, but her family came from Monterrey, Mexico. They immigrated to the United States when the cartel began persecuting the families there.

"She was visiting a friend in Napa. I met her at a harvest celebration dance. For me, it was love at first sight. I immediately went to her to ask her to dance. I'm a pretty good dancer, and I knew Maria would fall for my fancy feet." He laughed.

"I even sang to her while we danced. When some other fellow tapped my shoulder to dance with her, I said no. She seemed to like that. We danced and talked all night. I proposed to Maria that night!"

Luigi added, "Maria says that Charlie swept her off her feet. She said yes, and that is how we were so lucky to have Charlie Gee Vineyard Consulting in the Brazos Bottom."

Charlie smiled with a chuckle as he looked lovingly across the yard to his Maria.

I went over to introduce myself. She was full of light—so kind, so humble. I could see why Charlie was smitten. But I never believed in love at first sight, so I was curious about her perspective. I asked how she knew.

"My mother always told me that when I meet the one that God created for me, my soulmate, I would know. When I met Charlie, I knew." She pointed to her mom in heaven and said, "Mama was right."

As I walked back to Charlie and Luigi, I wondered if I would ever meet my soulmate. It seemed like such an unbelievable faith. I wondered out loud, "Why are farmers religious?"

Charlie heard me and responded, "Well, our very existence is so dependent on weather. You must have a belief in the Almighty to make it day to day. Families who live on the farm are usually close. They eat together, work together, and pray together. It is a hard life, but a gratifying one. Most farmers wouldn't trade their lifestyle for any other. There's nothing like the smell of morning dew and the joy of harvest.

"Farmers' mornings start early as the sun rises in the east. Lunch is usually spent at home with the family. Every meal is a celebration of the Lord's blessings and gifts. A farmer has a unique appreciation for food. They realize the efforts that went into producing it. A farmer never throws out leftovers."

I asked, "Why?"

He said, "Once you realize how hard it is to produce food, you never take the food for granted. Food, like any gift, should be cherished."

Charlie reflected, "When it rains, you sometimes see farmers get out of their tractors and look up to the heavens and say a prayer of thanksgiving. There is a farmer's prayer about rain. It goes like this:

> *Dear Lord, shower my fields with your tears. Let those tears*
> *bring abundance to my crop so that it may serve Your will.*
> *In Christ's Name, Amen.*

"When a farmer pays off his farm mortgage, he usually gives thanks to the Lord and makes his will to divide his land among the children. In this way, the land stays in the family. Farmer families identify with the land. Many farmers have passed down the land for generations."

Luigi interjected, "Charlie Gee was one of the best vineyard experts in the United States. People from California to New York called him for advice. Charlie could walk into a vineyard, reach down for a handful of dirt, and smell the quality of the soil. He would check the color of the soil and observe the density of soil particles. His passion for plant nutrition, fertilization, spray programs, and harvest parameters led him to experiment with more natural alternatives."

Charlie thanked Luigi for the compliment and gave an example, "When I was planting a vineyard in Sonoma, I discovered the vineyard had a major deer problem despite the eight-foot perimeter deer fence. First, I tried a commercial spray made up of coyote urine. What a stink! After spraying, I went to town and noticed all my friends moved away from me quickly. The next day I showed up in the vineyard and three deer were standing there greeting me. I realized that not only did the spray not work, but if I kept using it, I would not have any friends.

"Then an Italian vineyard manager friend said, 'Charlie, if you want to get rid of deer, spray a mixture of garlic, cloves, and cinnamon around the vineyard.' That sounded much too easy, and I did not think it would work, but I decided to try it. I made a strong solution of the ingredients my friend suggested and sprayed the vineyard. Morning and night I checked the vineyard at the time and places the deer would normally come. There were no deer. After a month there were still no deer. It worked! I told my Italian friend that deer do not like Italian seasonings." We laughed.

In days gone by, most wineries also had vineyards. Today, many wineries have no vineyards. Those wineries often fail to understand the arduous work that goes into producing excellent grapes.

It was obvious that Charlie loved the land and the people who worked it. Many winemakers don't give enough credit to the vineyard. They don't realize great wine begins in the vineyard. Winemakers enhance the qualities that are derived in the vineyard. Together, their partnership is like a beautiful melody complementing a beautiful verse.

There is an old saying, "You can tell how good the wine from any given vineyard will be by the number of the winemaker's footprints in that vineyard's soil."

Chapter 8

"My family has had our land in California for many generations," shared Charlie, "and has been selling our grapes to the same family winery there ever since. That type of relationship was important for me, and I was able to find it with the Metocks here." I remembered that Dr. Johnson mentioned the Metocks, so I asked Charlie to tell me about them.

He obliged. "The Metock family came to the Brazos Bottom from Bingen, Germany, along the Rhine. They arrived in the Bottom and bought land from another German family. Jon Metock and his wife, Mertle, have two daughters. They are a hard-working family and attend the Church of Lutheran Confession in Brenham. The two daughters are Heidi and Isabel.

"Even though the girls are fraternal twins, they could not be more different. Isabel is an introvert. Heidi is an extrovert. Isabel has flowing blonde hair and dimples in her left cheek. She is a tall girl and as smart as a whip. She was a straight-A student. But she has a funny limp. Some people say it was from horseback riding when she was young. It never seems to get in the way of her work. Come to think of it, one leg is shorter than the other. Isabel is very respectful.

"Heidi was a wild child and not the best of students. She is a short woman with jet black hair. She would never get anywhere near a horse or a book. My son went to school with her, and they even dated for a while. She was too much for him to handle. Both girls have worked at the winery and in the vineyard since they were twelve. During high school, Heidi would come in on Saturdays and work in the winery.

"Their father, Jon, has bright red hair, is a good Lutheran, and very respectful. That is one of the reasons my family always sold our grapes to him. When Jon says he'll do something, you know he'll do it. He's a good Christian man and a good father to the girls."

I asked how they met.

"Jon met Mertle at a Lutheran dance." Charlie shook his head and chuckled, "He wasn't much of a dancer, but Mertle was smitten with his big smile and bright red hair. Mertle was as blonde as you could be and a great cook. She made the best strudel in the Bottom and would often bring sausage and cabbage to our home. The Metock family—a good family, one you can depend upon. They make delicious wine from my grapes."

I could tell Charlie was concerned about who was going to take over when Jon slowed down.

Charlie reflected, "Jon is going to have to decide which one of his daughters is to take over the winery when he retires. He knows the girls don't get along, so they both cannot run the winery. He had hoped that Isabel would run the winery and Heidi would oversee sales. That's a decision to be made later.

"After prohibition, the capacity of the winery was 30,000 gallons. The Mctock family took a seedling of the Lenoir grape and created a clone of Lenoir. Jon called it 'his favorite,' and later it was named Favorite. He helped form the Brazos Bottom Winemaker's Association. Members of each of the five family wineries meet together each month and discuss methods to improve winemaking in the Bottom. They share harvesters and pruning crews, and they buy vineyard supplies as a coop. They have always cooperated, but are fiercely competitive.

"Everything went well for years until Heidi and Isabel joined the group. They were the first women to join the group. Their presence changed the level of cooperation. The men tried to outperform the ladies. Despite the men's efforts, the ladies were smarter, more consistent, and more dedicated than their male counterparts. It raised the level of accountability on everyone."

I asked Charlie if he had ever watched Jon make his wines. Charlie responded, "I have been selling my grapes to Jon for so long that Jon gives me free access to the winery. I love his large wooden tanks that hold my grapes."

Charlie shared the processes he had observed. "Jon sets up two-inch by ten-inch wooden boards over the top of the fermentation tanks each morning and evening. He climbs on the ladder to the top of the tank and stands on those planks. He takes his punch-down tool, which is a large circular piece of wood attached to a long staff and uses it to push the skins down into the liquid. Once the skins are contacting the liquid, the color of the juice gets darker and there is greater extraction of flavor from the skins. After fifteen minutes of pushing down the skins, the tank is well mixed. Jon does this in the early morning and before he goes home for the day.

"Jon has always been a very hands-on winemaker. Every harvest day he is on the crush pad inspecting the grapes, pumping them into the stemmer crusher, and into the tanks. All of the wooden tanks are oak open-top fermenters. He punches down his reds two times per day.

"Jon is old school. Most winemakers pump over. Pumping over is when the winemaker uses a pump to take the red liquid from the racking valve and pump the juice over the top of the skins that have risen to the top, which are called the cap. Incorporation of the juice pumped over the cap extracts red color from the skins. Pumping over is an alternative to punching down which is manually pushing the cap down into the fermenting wine. He must climb up on the top of the tank and lean over the cap while pushing down with a flat ended tool. It takes strength and balance.

"He airs out the room before he enters because there is a lack of oxygen in the room due to the tanks having fermentation. Once the room is aired out, he enters the room and climbs on the top of the tank. Standing on top of the planks and pushing down the skins, each tank takes fifteen minutes. There are six tanks in the room."

Charlie continued, "Jon told me that business is so good that he hired an assistant. His neighbor's son, Fritz Blau, is a high school graduate from Brenham High School. Fritz was not a great student and did not go to college. He struggled with spelling. Fritz was diagnosed as dyslexic. It takes him a while to think of what he will say. And I swear that child cannot remember anyone's name.

"He is a kind and gentle soul from a good German family, and he's hard working. He catches on quickly, and Jon likes him a lot. Fritz and Isabel went to high school together and are friends. I have seen them together. If you ask me, there is romance in the air."

We thanked Charlie for his time and wandered off to check out the gambling. Gambling in the Brazos Bottom is like a trip to downtown Las Vegas. There are blackjack tables and real craps tables. The dealers wear uniforms and the wine flows. Thousands of dollars cross the tables. Real chips are used, and the bank is the Bank of the Brazos Bottom.

Luigi explained, "Often, winery families secure a line of credit in advance and settle-up at the end of the night. Occasionally the family will lose more than they can cover, so they pay a visit to the bank the next day. The Nizzi and Galle families often pay a visit to the bank the next day."

I wanted to watch Mr. Nizzi after hearing Charlie talk about his time sleeping in the pickup truck and promising he would never gamble again. Luigi said, "I guess he forgot about his promise to quit gambling."

We found Mr. Nizzi at the craps table. He was on a roll. The lady standing next to me said he started with $1,000 in chips. The table was cheering because he had rolled three sevens in a row.

Luigi whispered to me, "It looks like he has $4,000 in front of him. That puts him up $3,000. He should walk away now." He rolled again. It was a four.

"That is the most difficult point to hit," said Luigi as he coached me in the game. Mr. Nizzi rolled again and again, adding bets on five, six, eight and nine. The guests at the table were cheering him on. He rolled crap twelve, and then crap two.

Luigi leaned over and said, "That is usually good luck, since he has his bets already on the table." Mr. Nizzi had bet all $4,000.

The next roll flew off the table. Everyone at the table groaned, including Luigi. I asked what happened.

He said, "That is unusually bad luck."

Mr. Nizzi cried out, "I want the same dice." He bragged, "I am ready to hit this point and then hit the other numbers. Then I will quit for the night." I told Luigi that Mr. Nizzi should leave now.

Mr. Nizzi shook and shook the dice and rolled them straight down the middle of the table. The first dice hit the wall on the end and settled, exposing three. He needed a nine, five, eight, or six. He did not want the second dice to be a four. The second dice hit the wall and flew straight up in the air. It landed and rolled around, finally landing, and exposing a four. Everyone at the table let out a painful groan. It felt like the air left the area. Mr. Nizzi rolled a seven and lost all $4,000—his original $1,000 and the $3,000 he had won. I told Luigi, "I can only imagine how upset Mrs. Nizzi will be."

Luigi chuckled. "It looks like Mr. Nizzi will be sleeping in his pickup truck again. Money is won and lost every night of gambling."

Chapter 9

The next day Luigi and I went to the Metock Winery. Two men were having a very serious conversation when we arrived. From what we could overhear, the two men were Jon Metock and the young man Fritz, who Charlie had said was a friend of Isabel.

The older man who I identified as Jon was saying, "Fritz, you have been a good employee. But since your friendship with Isabel has turned into a romance, it is affecting your work performance."

I could tell Fritz was angry. His fists were clenched, and his arms were crossed. He looked away when Jon said, "I want you to stop seeing my daughter Isabel. I will talk with her as well. And Fritz, do you have the pickers lined up for harvest on August tenth?"

Fritz hesitated. He knew that if he talked back to Jon, Jon would fire him on the spot. Fritz did have a high school reputation for getting into fights. Then, staring down at his feet, he responded, "Yes, sir."

I could see that Fritz was embarrassed and his face was red. He stormed off quietly. I would have felt betrayed to be scolded in front of anyone, especially if I was a loyal employee. Winery work is hard and tiring. You must really be committed and have a passion for it.

When Jon noticed us, he left Fritz and came over to introduce himself. We told him about our meeting with Charlie Gee and how complimentary Charlie had been. Jon seemed pleased, "Charlie and his family have been good friends for many years. Welcome to our winery. I am sorry you heard that interaction. Fritz has been such a blessing to me in the winery, but he seems distracted."

Jon showed us around the winery and invited us to lunch at his home. Mertle greeted us like we were long lost family. Isabel and Heidi joined us as well. Isabel was very polite. Heidi was full of questions. After sharing our life stories, Heidi encouraged us to join in the harvest this year.

Jon called Isabel into the next room while we spoke with Heidi. Heidi leaned toward us and said quietly, "Dad is telling Isabel to break it off with Fritz." We really felt like part of the family then.

Jon and Isabel came back to the table. Her eyes were red like she had been crying. Isabel was silent during the meal, and she kept her head down as though to avoid conversation.

Lunch was delicious and the strudel for dessert was heavenly. I asked for the recipe. Mertle seemed pleased and gave me a copy.

Mertle's Strudel

Ingredients

- 1 package frozen phyllo dough (thawed)
- ¾ cup raisins, hydrated in ½ cup Messina Hof Angel Riesling for about 30 minutes
- 2 large (or 3 to 4 medium sized) Granny Smith apples
- 1 tablespoon lemon juice
- 1 teaspoon cinnamon
- ½ cup sugar
- 8 tablespoons (1 stick + 1 tablespoon) unsalted butter, melted

- Powdered sugar

Directions

1. Place phyllo dough in the refrigerator to thaw the night before you plan to make the strudel.

2. Preheat the oven to 350 degrees F.

3. Peel and core the apples. Chop into pieces about ½ inch thick cubed.

4. Drain raisins. Reserve liquid.

5. Transfer apples to a bowl along with the raisins, followed by the lemon juice, 1 tablespoon of the reserved Angel wine, cinnamon, and sugar. Stir to combine.

6. Unfold and separate the phyllo dough into 10 individual sheets (cover them with a damp kitchen towel to keep them from drying out while you work).

7. Line baking sheet with parchment paper cut to fit. Lightly sprinkle with all-purpose flour and lay the first phyllo sheet down.

8. Using a pastry brush, coat the first sheet of pastry with a light sheen of butter, and sprinkle with sugar. Repeat with the remaining sheets of phyllo, leaving the final sheet uncoated.

9. Evenly sprinkle apple mixture, running the bottom length of the pastry. Fold the edges over the filling and roll carefully to put the seam-side down.

10. Brush with melted butter and bake until the pastry is deeply golden and begins to flake, about 40 minutes.

11. Sift powdered sugar over the top and serve with Bluebell Homemade vanilla ice cream.

Conversation at the table drifted to the wine family relationships. Heidi expressed concern about the BonderKisty family winery. She said, "They control a lot of the grapes in the Bottom. With the issues of the Kisty boy hurting Rose Galle and their problems in the vineyard, the winery seems distracted. It could impact all of us."

Luigi asked what problems were in the vineyard. Heidi replied, "They are dying."

I asked her to tell us more. Dead vineyards can kill a wine industry. "Contact Mr. Bonder. He can tell you about it," she replied.

We thanked them for their hospitality and went to see Mr. Bonder at BonderKisty. As we drove into the winery estate, we saw a man in the vineyard. "Hello," Luigi said. "Can you tell us where we would find Mr. Bonder?"

The man looked at us and asked who we were. We talked to him, and he introduced himself as Greg Bonder. "I am the owner here. What can I do for you?"

I looked at the leaf deformations in the vineyard and told him, "I am familiar with chemical damage in vines from my experience in the High Plains. I would like to help you."

After much conversation, he said, "Trevor, I would like for you to investigate the death of these five acres of vineyard. The vines were doing fine. They have always produced fantastic fruit and wonderful wine. When the spring rains stimulated growth, the vines began to decline. As the young clusters developed, they began to fall off the plant. Then the leaves began to fall off.

"I contacted the Texas Department of Agriculture, but they were no help. They came out to investigate but only investigated me. They found that I had a lapse in my spray license and fined me $2,000. They did take samples and confirmed dicamba herbicide damage on the leaves. I expected them to survey the surrounding farmers' fields, but they did nothing."

I recognized those symptoms but said nothing. I told him I would let him know what I found. After collecting soil samples and leaf samples, I took them to the Texas A&M pathology lab. They ran the tests and found traces of dicamba in the soil and found leaf symptoms consistent with dicamba spray. Luigi and I started surveying the surrounding fields and discovered the cotton farmer to the south had sprayed dicamba in preparation of his cotton planting.

Luigi asked me why that was important. I told him that if the wind is blowing more than ten miles per hour, and if the temperature is over 90 degrees Fahrenheit, dicamba will drift to other fields. In fact, it will continue to be present and volatize days later to drift in whatever direction the wind may blow.

Bayer Chemical owns the dicamba seeds. They received Environmental Protection Agency approval based on conditions that do not exist normally in Texas. Here, the wind rarely blows less than ten miles per hour, and the temperature is rarely under 90 degrees Fahrenheit when dicamba herbicide is sprayed on the cotton fields. Cotton fields dominate the majority of Brazos Bottom farmland.

Luigi became a crusader. "We need to take this evidence to the Texas Department of Agriculture." We did, but nothing happened. I reported back to Mr. Bonder all that I knew and which farmer I felt was the source of the dicamba. He thanked me for trying.

Several days later, Mr. Bonder reached out to me to share, "I went to visit the cotton farmer, Elway Tow, to discuss his spraying. I thought we could have a neighborly conversation. I knocked on the door and Elway opened the door. I was not invited in, and the conversation went very badly. Elway told me to get off his property and that cotton has been growing on his land for generations. He even said that vineyards were not meant to be grown in the Brazos Bottom."

"This is not good news," Luigi told me after we left Mr. Bonder. "There will be a war between the Bonders, Kristys and Tows now. Elway Tow is a third-generation cotton farmer who is not a fan of grape farmers. He remembers the good ol' days when aerial spraying was common. Now ground spraying is required."

It made me sad that neighbors could not work together for the good of all, so I tried to intervene. Surely, I thought, the farmers just do not understand this chemical, and I could educate them.

When I went to visit Mr. Tow, he was very cordial and invited me into his home. I thought perhaps Mr. Bonder may have approached him more harshly. Mr. Tow and I sat and talked for an hour.

I asked him how much he knew about dicamba, and he responded, "The chemical company tells us when to use it. I read the label to see on what crops I can use it."

"Did you know that dicamba herbicide cannot be sprayed when the wind is blowing above ten miles per hour?" He looked a little surprised but did not respond.

I went on to share that it was preferable to spray when the wind was not blowing from the south. He said, "Go on."

"Dicamba herbicide should not be sprayed when the temperature exceeds 90 degrees Fahrenheit because the spray volatizes and drifts from the cotton field to the vineyard.

Mr. Tow thought about what I said and replied, "You know that with those restrictions it is virtually impossible to spray, right? The bottom line is that cotton farmers must get the crops to market. We were here long before grapes. Grapes do not belong in the Brazos Bottom."

He continued, "When Greg Bonder showed up at my door notifying me of his herbicide damaged vineyard and his request for an investigation by the Texas Department of Agriculture, I was afraid of a lawsuit and fines. I even organized other cotton farmers to be at the county council when we had to defend our rights and prevent restrictions of dicamba use."

Mr. Tow later said that my visit made him realize his cotton crop could be compatible with his neighbor's vineyard if they coordinated.

I was incredibly pleased with myself. I had deflated a hot conflict between the cotton farmer and the grape grower. In other states, this conflict resulted in murders and violence. I felt like I had calmed the waters of neighborly love.

Chapter 10

All was calm until the cotton farmer sprayed dicamba herbicide to eliminate weeds in his dicamba-ready cotton. Within a week, Greg Bonder once again saw leaf symptoms in his vineyard closest to Mr. Tow's cotton field. It appeared Mr. Tow sprayed when it was 95 degrees Fahrenheit and the wind blew first from the south, then the wind shifted, and blew from the west. This time many wine growers were affected. The Texas Department of Agriculture was called. The agent in the area was on vacation. She would not be back for two weeks. Leaf symptoms showed up in all of the Brazos Bottom vineyards.

One week later, cotton farmer Elway Tow was found dead with his throat cut in the cab of his tractor. A bloody harvest knife was found on the floor of the cab. Sergeant Jeffries came out to investigate and discovered the harvest knife was the type used by grape growers. He called me to help him.

Sergeant Jeffries posed the question, "Which grape grower killed Elway Tow, or was it some other neighboring cotton farmer trying to set up a grape grower as the murderer?"

I replied, "Both cotton growers and grape growers can be harmed by the spray, so it could have been either. Cotton farmers are at war with each other. Some cotton farmers use dicamba-ready seed. Some farmers use 2-4D-ready seed. Some farmers grow cotton organically."

The sergeant asked, "What do you mean by 'ready seed'?" I explained that if a seed was 'ready' for a particular chemical, it meant the plant had been genetically altered so that the chemical no longer affected it. He summarized, "So, you're saying that dicamba cannot kill a plant from a dicamba-ready seed and 2-4D cannot kill a plant from a 2-4D ready seed?"

"Yes, you're correct, but dicamba can kill a plant from a 2-4D-ready seed and vice versa. Cotton farmers that are organic can have their cotton crop killed by dicamba, 2-4D, or Roundup."

Sergeant Jeffries then noticed the initials "PG" carved in the handle of the bloody harvest knife.

The sergeant started interviewing vineyard managers. He looked for initials that matched the harvest knife. As it turned out, two of the vineyard managers matched the initials. Sergeant Jeffries called both managers in. One was Peter Galle; the other was Paul Gilbert. Both managers claimed to be at the Unified Wine meeting in Sacramento at the time of the death.

Sergeant Jeffries thought he had come to a dead end. "Thank you, gentlemen. I appreciate you taking the time to come in. Peter, have you lost a harvest knife?" Peter responded, "I don't have mine right now. I loaned it to a cotton farmer, Jess Crass, who has a small vineyard. Jess told me that he had offered to buy Elway's land, but Elway refused.

"Jess Crass is new to the Brazos Bottom. He was a wheat farmer in Washington State. He moved his family to the Brazos Bottom only six months ago. He had wanted land to purchase and was anxious to be one of the largest grape growers in the area."

Sergeant Jeffries phoned Jess Crass for an interview, but no one answered the phone. Peter offered to go with Sergeant

Jeffries to Jess's house, since it may have been his knife that was found. When they arrived at the Crass house, Mrs. Crass told them that she had not seen Jess since breakfast. "Thank you, ma'am," Sergeant Jeffries said politely. "Do you mind if I look around the property?" "No," she said, "please feel free."

They went into the barn and found Jess in his pickup truck with the engine on. Sergeant Jeffries realized at once that Jess had tried to kill himself with carbon monoxide poisoning, so he ripped open the truck door, turned off the engine, and pulled Jess's lifeless body out into the fresh air.

He told Peter to call an ambulance while he gave Jess mouth-to-mouth resuscitation. It was too late. Jess was dead. The ambulance crew made the final pronouncement when they arrived.

Upon further inspection of the truck, Sergeant Jeffries found a suicide note written by Jess.

> *Dear Lord, please forgive me. I have sinned dreadfully. I killed a man for my own greed. I was overcome with anger when I offered to buy his cotton land and he turned me down. I thought that I could convince his widow to sell the farm since Elway was dead.*

> *I sinned against Peter Galle by casting blame on him with his harvest knife that I borrowed. Please tell Peter that I am sorry. I am thankful he was at the Unified Symposium and can clear his name.*

> *Please forgive me for being a coward. I could not face any of these people that I have hurt. When I heard the Sergeant*

was interviewing the managers, I knew the truth would be revealed and I would be found out.

I sinned against my wife. Please forgive me for abandoning you. I did not want to bring disgrace to you and the family. It is better for you than a lengthy expensive trial.

Sergeant Jeffries visited with Jess Crass's wife and shared Jess's suicide note with her. She sat in silence staring at him and Peter. Her eyes never blinked. Sergeant Jeffries suggested that Peter wait for him in the car. The Sergeant sat with Mrs. Crass in silence. He offered her something to drink. She shook her head no. As he sat there looking around the house, he realized that there was very little furniture. The Crass's had moved to the Brazos Bottom with the dream of being grape growers and had spent all their money on the move. They had nothing.

Mrs. Crass was helpless and hopeless. She did not see this coming. She looked at Sergeant Jeffries and asked, "What do I do now?"

Sergeant Jeffries consoled her and told her that he would get some local ladies to help her. He and Peter talked about it as they drove back to the office. Peter volunteered to get his family involved.

Peter came from a big Italian family and even bigger Italian community. As soon as he told his mother about Mrs. Crass, his mother called all her friends, relatives, and the church.

Peter's mother brought their family to Mrs. Crass's home with enough food for a week. They encouraged her to stay and offered to help with labor, grapes, and equipment to fulfill the dream that had brought them to the area. Peter remembered Sergeant Jeffries wife worked at the local Food Bank, so he called Fatama asking for help. Fatama came to the house the same day bearing gifts of food to fill Mrs. Crass's pantry. They also told Mrs. Crass that if she decided to leave, they understood and would help her sell her property. Mrs. Galle told her that her husband Alfonse had connections and would be happy to help.

Sergeant Jeffries was relieved that the murder was solved before the wine families' meeting and there was no other animosity with the cotton farmers.

Chapter 11

Harvest in the Bottom was only one week away. Jon Metock invited me to an annual meeting of the families to discuss how the Brazos Bottom Harvester would be shared and scheduled. I accepted; I was so interested in how that worked.

Jon explained, "The wine families went together to purchase a modern harvester. It is the latest model and very expensive. It cost us $300,000." I asked who operated it.

Jon told me, "The operator for the past five years has been Felix Bolt. He's a likeable guy, but unfortunately Felix is a drinker. He likes his bourbon. Each day he drinks a fifth of Bourbon and then wakes up the next morning ready to harvest. He's never missed a row.

"He also smokes three packs of cigarettes a day. When he operates the harvester, we can barely see him in the cloud of cigarette smoke. He's been in jail serving a six-month sentence after his third DWI. That hurts us because he's so good at working the harvester and is very flexible. Felix removes the fruit without damaging the vines."

At the meeting, the leader was Greg Bonder. He reported, "The families begged the county judge to release Felix during the day so he could support his family if he would return to jail at night. We promised that we would monitor Felix and make sure he complied with the judge's instructions. The County Judge is a staunch supporter of the Brazos Bottom wineries, so he accepted our proposal to place Felix on a work release."

The families all seemed to be pleased with this report. They immediately gathered around a table where Isabel Metock created a ledger for scheduling the harvest by vineyard and grape type.

Later Jon reported to me that Felix was fine for the first day in the Bonder vineyard. The second day, Felix was to harvest Ben Kisty's grapes for the BonderKisty Winery, but Felix couldn't be found. Ben got in his Polaris and drove through the neighboring vineyards to see if Felix was working elsewhere. Ben found him sitting in the harvester drunk as a skunk. He took Felix back to his home, where he and his wife sobered Felix up and took him back to the county jail.

Ben sent out a follow-up email to all the families alerting them to evaluate Felix before he went back to the jail so he would not flunk their breathalyzer. Felix worked the rest of the week, but the last day he flunked, so the judge revoked his work release.

Ben sent an email with updated instructions. He wrote, "Felix is lost for the harvest season. His son, Jeremy, who is twenty years old, knows how to drive the harvester. Felix taught him. Jeremy lives at home, so he can support his mom. He visits his dad in the county jail. They need the money, and we need someone who can drive the harvester." Jeremy was hired.

Jon shared, "Jeremy is a straight-A student. He even received a scholarship to Harvard but deferred until the harvest was over. He is a wonderful young man. He told his mom that he would support her while Felix was in jail. He is the model son."

On one evening, Jeremy ran the harvester through the vine rows when the rods broke. Jeremy was able to put them back together and continue the harvesting.

I ran into Charlie Gee again and told him about Felix. He already knew and just shook his head. He said, "There's always drama at harvest. Did you hear about the Metocks?" I was surprised and said that I had just seen Jon at the family's harvester meeting, and Jon said nothing.

Charlie updated me. "Do you remember what I said about Isabel and Fritz?" I recalled that Charlie thought there might be romance and I remembered the conversation between Jon and Isabel at lunch.

Charlie continued, "Jon did not suspect a thing. Then last night Jon took his tractor to the far corner of the vineyard to change the water on the irrigation system. In the distance he could see a car; it was a pickup that looked a lot like Fritz's. As he approached the pickup, the Ford F-150 sped off.

"Jon spoke to Isabel and asked if she was in Fritz's pickup. She denied being with Fritz and swore she had not seen Fritz since her father had spoken to her. Fritz also denied he was in the vineyard. Jon became very suspicious. Isabel has been noticeably quieter since that incident. It is like ice between Isabel and her father. She talks to her mother but does not have much to say to her dad.

"It is a shame," he sighed, "because Isabel always had open communication with Jon. Now Isabel acts like she is withholding a secret. I think Jon can sense Isabel's dishonesty.

"Now, Isabel's sister, Heidi, works very closely with her dad. His trust in Heidi seems to have grown. She complains to him about Fritz's work performance and says it is getting worse. He is sloppy. The winery is not clean, and their harvest is only one week away. Jon told me that Fritz has been coming in late and leaving early. This year will be a big crop. Everything must go with good German precision. We will see what happens."

I asked how Jon and Mertle were doing. "Are they having financial problems?"

Charlie thoughtfully responded. "Jon lives a good life. He built a new home. He took his wife to France and Germany on trips that he called information-collecting trips. He and Mertle have been having problems since the incident occurred with Isabel. Jon started blaming Mertle for interfering. It got so bad that Jon now sleeps in the second bedroom. He is miserable and says this has never happened in their marriage. Up until now, Jon and Mertle have had a perfect marriage."

"How is his health? Worry and turmoil can bring you down," I commented.

"I know Jon is worried about the upcoming harvest, and it is affecting his personality," said Charlie. "I don't believe Jon feels he can trust any of his workers. Now he depends more on Heidi."

Luigi and I were scheduled to help pick on August tenth. We were looking forward to it. Then on August ninth I got a call from Heidi saying, "The pick is off! Fritz totally forgot to get the pickers. Dad asked him this morning how many pickers he had, and Fritz turned white. His speech stuttered and finally he had to admit that he forgot to call them. Dad was furious. We have rescheduled the pick for August seventeenth. Can you come?"

"Of course," I said. "We'll be there to help."

I was concerned about Jon, so I called him to ask how things were going. Jon answered the phone with anguish in his voice. I asked him if he was okay. "Not well, Trevor," he said. "I had to tell Fritz today that if he screwed up one more time, he is fired. Fritz looks at me with hatred in his eyes. I do not know what I am going to do. I have asked Heidi to secure a picking crew, since Fritz messed up the first week of harvest."

I was surprised to hear him say that. Normally, Isabel would have been his go-to person. Jon had such confidence in Isabel, and Isabel was so committed to the winery. I became concerned. Now Heidi had to step up, and I hoped she was ready.

Jon went on, "You know, Trevor, when you delay harvest a week, you get overripe fruit with reduced tonnage. You also run the risk of rain. Fritz really screwed up this time."

The day before harvest, August the sixteenth, I ran into Fritz. We talked briefly, and I could tell he was truly angry with Heidi, since he had been passed over to secure the pickers. It could be an interesting harvest. "Would you and Luigi like to join us?" asked Fritz. I told him that we had promised Jon and his family we would be there to help.

Charlie, too, reached out to see if we would be coming. He said his family would be there and asked if we had heard the latest. Luigi looked eager, and I was fascinated with the story, so we said no; what was the latest?

Charlie continued, "Heidi drove to Cat Springs and enlisted 30 harvest pickers. They are to show up at daylight on August the seventeenth, and she hopes that all the picking will be done by 3:00 p.m. That's enough time so that they can process the grapes and clean up the winery after harvest. She's really coming on strong."

Chapter 12

Luigi picked me up while it was still dark. It was his first time to pick. I could feel his energy and excitement. I felt right at home from harvest in the Texas High Plains when I lived there.

Harvest is a celebration, yet it's high pressure. Machines need to work. Growers need to communicate. The skies need to stay clear. The grape growers pray:

Dear Lord, let Your skies be clear. Let Your tears stay dry. Let the wind blow to keep us cool.

We all arrived in the vineyard just before sunrise - such a beautiful time of the day. We could hear the birds singing, smell the earth, and touch the very ripe fruit. Charlie and his family were there. He greeted us and made an introduction. Jon thanked us all for coming to pick.

We began picking. It is amazing to see the coordinated rhythm of the pickers working their way down the vine row. Many of the pickers sang as they picked. One picker caught my eye. She was working hard, but she was smiling and talking like it was a day at the beach. Everyone else seemed serious, focused, and quiet. That is, everyone except those who were next to her.

Heidi saw me. "Hi, Trevor. Have you met Lulu?"

"No. Lulu who?" I said nonchalantly, like I had no idea what she was saying.

"Lulu, the cute girl smiling and talking while she's picking. You know, the one you keep staring at?"

I'm sure I blushed. "No, I haven't met Lulu."

"Let me introduce you," she said. "Come with me."

We walked over to the next row, and Heidi introduced us. Lulu gave me a big, "Howdy!" and stuck out her purple, grape-stained hand to shake mine.

I asked, "Are you an Aggie?"

"Yes," she said proudly. "I'm a graduate student in plant pathology working on my PhD. Would you like to pick with me?"

We picked and talked and talked and picked. She had the same love of Texas grapes and wine that I did.

Luigi, smiling, called my name. "Trevor, why don't you give us men a hand with the lugs?"

The stronger men of the picker group lifted the overflowing harvest lugs and carried them to the half-ton harvest containers, where they gave them to the dumpers. The dumpers lifted the lugs above their heads and dumped the grapes from the lugs into large titan bins. They all looked strong and had large biceps.

Luigi and I looked at each other and quickly volunteered to be in the strong pickers group. The pickers were moving faster than normal. Luigi and I were hustling. The dumpers had difficulty keeping up with the pickers. As the day wore on, you could see the sweat on the brow of each of the pickers and dumpers. Luigi and I were soaked. The torrid sun beat down on us as we picked. The sun ripens the fruit, but bakes the pickers.

When the vineyard was finally picked, the pickers and the dumpers celebrated with a drink of last year's wines, plus food specially prepared that day by each family's kitchen. Mertle made Treberwurst. She packed sausages and bratwursts in the first week's must and marinated them all week. At the end of today's pick, she roasted them and served them with mustard and crusty breads. She said it was a tradition from her homeland.

I made my way back to Lulu. Her joyful personality amazed me. I felt a little lightheaded around her and wondered if I was overheated. No one else seemed to have that condition. "Is this your first harvest?" I asked.

She laughed and said no. "I'm from California. My family had a vineyard there, and I was raised in it. I've done many harvests and every other activity in the vineyard. That's why plant pathology is so important to me."

"How did you get to Texas A&M University?" I asked.

"I have an uncle who went to school there. He raved about it and even invited me to a football game once. It was such an unbelievable experience, I knew I had to be an Aggie," she laughed.

As the group enjoyed wine and fellowship, three of the pickers brought out guitars and began playing and singing. People started clapping and dancing and singing along. It was a joyous celebration.

Then, Lulu asked me to dance. I tried to explain that I did not dance, but she grabbed my hand and pulled me toward the music, laughing as she tried to teach me the steps.

As I tried to follow her feet movements and listen to the music, I watched her. She had such a joyful soul. I had never met anyone with such a positive approach to life. My first dancing experience did not go so well, so I asked Lulu if we could try again at a later date. She laughed and said it would be one of her new challenges.

Exhausted, I had to sit down. She kept dancing. Charlie came and sat beside me.

He shared, "This day's plan went flawlessly. Twelve tons of grapes were picked. Twelve tons produce 2,700 gallons of red grape-must."

Must is the skin and juice created by the crush of the grapes. I was impressed and told him so. "Charlie, that was a good yield for the twelve tons. You produce very juicy grapes."

"Yes," he replied, "and that's without irrigation. Jon doesn't want me to irrigate before harvest. When it's harvest time, the grape farmer prays for sunny days and no rain. Usually, the first thing a grape farmer does when he awakes is to check the weather. The last thing the grape farmer does before going to bed is check the weather. My grapes have deep roots. My grapes are juicy."

He paused and qualified his answer.

"There are good vintages and bad vintages. I remember a few years back when I was managing a beautiful crop of Blanc Du Bois here in the Bottom. The vineyard had consistently produced gold medal wines. There was a storm in the Gulf, and I knew I had to harvest fast.

"Thirty pickers were in the vineyard ready to go. The black clouds were coming in from the south. The refrigerated truck had broken down and could not be used. I got my trailer and loaded the bins on it.

"I pulled up to the vineyard and the pickers were working feverishly. They filled the first trailer load, which was offloaded and processed at the winery. I drove ninety miles per hour back to the Bottom. The picking was completed, and the fruit made it to the winery. Just as the trailer pulled away from the vineyard, a hailstorm started."

Luigi bragged, "Charlie was the hero, if he had not acted so fast, the crop would have been lost. That Blanc Du Bois won the International Award for excellence in Vienna, Austria. The story spread through the Bottom. He saved the crop. Every vineyard worker wants to work with Charlie. He is the local vineyard mentor."

I congratulated Charlie with a nod and then looked around. The dancing had stopped, and Lulu was gone. I felt foolish that I didn't get her last name, but I reminded myself that Heidi could tell me. Lulu so impressed me. Her smile, her joy, and enthusiasm were contagious. She made all the pickers around her work faster without her asking them to work harder. Her example and joy made it fun to pick in the daytime heat.

Just thinking about seeing her again made me look forward to our next dance lesson and the opportunity to spend more time around her joyful soul.

My mother's one-liner 'there is a lid for every pot' came to mind. Could Lulu be my 'lid' – my soulmate? Maybe I was just imagining things. Maybe I was making too much of this.

Chapter 13

Charlie's voice interrupted my thoughts, "The production team has their work cut out for them," he said. "They're responsible for processing this bountiful harvest. The pickers' work is done, the production workers' work has just begun."

You can always tell a fantastic vintage by the bees. They are in the vineyard when you pick. They are on the grapes as they are transported to the crush pad. They stay on the grapes even as the grapes are elevated into the stemmer crusher. Then they swarm to the next harvest bin.

As the grapes are crushed, there is a familiar aroma of sweet grape juice and whatever fruit character is reminiscent to that variety. When we harvest muscat, the air is filled with the aroma of peaches. When we harvest Lenoir, the air is filled with the aroma of chocolate cherries. Each variety has its distinctive aroma.

Most of the vineyards practiced sustainable agriculture minimizing use of chemicals that hurt the environment. There are so many beneficial spiders and insects—bees, wasps, and dragonflies—in the vineyard.

I have also noticed that when you see a dove or quail nest in the vine, you see a full crop of grapes surrounding the nest. Mama birds are so smart to build their nests near an easy food source. It is amazing to see the cooperation within nature. It is such a blessing.

Jon told Luigi, "The red grapes bleed a blood-red. Since we picked these grapes one week later than normal, the grapes were even darker. As the grapes transfer through the crusher, the pump transports the grapes to the tank. As the grapes enter the tank, the aroma explodes. The grape skins and juice integrate to marry. After two weeks of grape skin and juice integration, the wine color is black."

I remembered from days at Equoni, the winery in west Texas where I worked while I taught at Texas Tech, that next we pressed off the skins. The skins, once they're pressed off, are composted and replaced into the vineyard. This year the Metock Winery is collaborating with a pig farmer who is buying the skin and grape-must to feed his pigs. Grape-must is a wonderful source of vitamins, fiber, and sugar for pig feed. Pigs are very choosy about their feed. When grape-must skins are rotated with normal pig food, the pigs seem to thrive. We have thus found another use of grape skins, post press.

Jon added, "Once the grapes skins are pressed off the wine, the wine continues to ferment until all the grape sugar has been converted to alcohol. I want to thank you both for your help and support."

Jon made a point to visit every worker to show his gratitude. I watched as he made the rounds.

Most were leaving. Only Luigi and I were left. Jon shared, "This vintage is outstanding, and most of the wines will be 14% alcohol. After settling the juice for eight weeks, the wine will be ready to go into barrels."

The barrels Jon uses are French/American hybrids. 50% of the barrels are French Oak and 50% of the barrels are American Oak. French oak supplies the finesse of the wine, and American oak supplies the aggressive oak flavors. Winemaking is an art and a science. I was amazed to learn there are 2500 decisions that winemakers make for each vintage.

I asked Jon if I could work with him in the winery.

He looked at me and cocked his head toward the cellar and said, "It is time to punch down the tank from the first harvest day for the second time. You are welcome to help. I will be here for a while. My wife never expects me home until 10:00 p.m., because after I do the punch downs, I return to the lab and perform all the wine chemistry. You are welcome to watch."

He checked the grape-must sugar content and the grape-must pH and acidity. He then adjusted the grape-must. Those adjustments could be a little bit more acid or a little bit more sugar to make the grape-must have a higher alcohol content. I asked him what adjustments he was going to make.

He replied, "None needed on the grapes we harvested today. Their chemistry is perfect."

He then recorded all the entries into the lab book, and I helped him clean up before going home. On his way out, he made sure that the tank temperatures were set, and the crush pad equipment was sanitized and ready to receive grapes on the next harvest day.

I asked him when the next harvest day would be. He said, "The next harvest day will be August the twentieth. Heidi will again secure the harvest crew."

The days flew by. I was as anxious to see Lulu again as I was to participate in the pick.

Luigi and I joined the thirty pickers from Cat Springs who arrived at 7:00 a.m. It was another successful harvest day. Jon congratulated the staff and the pickers that afternoon. Twelve more tons were picked. I looked for Lulu but did not see her.

I worked my way over to Heidi and asked about Lulu. "I thought she would be picking."

Heidi responded, "Lulu could not pick because she had a lot of schoolwork." She looked at me sternly. "Trevor, do not tell me that you did not ask Lulu for her number." I looked down at the ground. She felt my pain and gave me the number. I promised I would call.

This pick filled the second 3,500-gallon tank. The processing went extremely well. Tank number one had begun to ferment. The harvest season was off to a great start. Isabel and Heidi helped pick and assisted in the winery.

I could see that Jon was always incredibly careful. Safety and cleanliness are his highest priorities. He told the girls, "In the tank room there is a faint amount of carbon dioxide filling the fermentation room. Be careful. We will have to open the door thirty minutes before punch-down. If there is a lot of carbon dioxide in the room, remember that means there is very little oxygen. Too much CO_2 in the fermentation room is extremely dangerous. CO_2 is a colorless and odorless gas. It displaces oxygen. It can lead to dizziness, loss of consciousness, and death. It can produce a burning sensation in the nose. CO_2 normally accumulates in the lower part of the room. Airing the room out makes it safe." Jon said good night and went home. Luigi and I left feeling like we were a part of this family and the wine.

Chapter 14

The next day Jon told me, "Later last night I was called to the emergency room at St. Theresa Hospital. The doctor said my daughter Heidi's car had been run off the road and she was in a coma."

I was stunned and offered to help. He said that the police were investigating and were convinced this was no accident.

"She was deliberately run off the road," he said. "The best witness is Heidi, and she is in a coma." I asked who was covering the case. He said a Detective Larry wanted to speak to him.

I told him that I was happy to go with him. "Thank you, Trevor, I would appreciate your being there."

We learned that Detective Larry was new to the Brenham Police Department and that he had previously been working for the FBI. He retired to Brenham to be near his ninety-five-year-old mother. She lives with him and his wife, Ann. They had been living in Annapolis, Maryland, and had been doing background checks for incoming Naval Academy cadets and faculty. Detective Larry was quite familiar with interrogation and was very perceptive.

One of the police officers said, "The town is very lucky to have such an experienced investigator. His nose for uncovering crime is amazing. He asks questions that seem harmless, yet they always lead to more follow-up." Detective Larry sounded like a bloodhound.

Detective Larry asked if Jon believed that there was someone who would like to kill Heidi.

Jon said, "Heidi and Isabel did not get along. I know they love each other, but they also hate each other.

"Heidi recently broke up with her longtime boyfriend Martin Sanderson. Martin is from a German family that has been in Brenham for generations. His grandfather was from Hof, Germany, and he was a bricklayer.

"His grandfather was Otto and was from a stone mason family in Hof. He came to Brenham for greater opportunities. Otto was a silver haired Santa-looking man who was known throughout the Bottom as the best stone mason. He even played Santa in the Brazos Bottom Christmas Parade.

"The family also came from a long line of beer masters. Otto loved making his beer. When he would come on a masonry job, he always brought a stein of his best brew. Martin got his love of beer from his dad and grandfather's home beer brewing. Martin followed in their profession of stone masons."

Jon said, "I was surprised that they broke up. When I asked Heidi before the accident why they broke up, she said it was complicated and really did not want to talk about it."

Detective Larry said that everyone was a suspect because no one was obvious.

Jon and I went to the scene of the accident. There were tire tracks of two cars. One was obviously Heidi's. The tire tracks of the second vehicle were that of a Ford F-150. Unfortunately, that was the most common pickup truck in Brenham. There was a collision, and there was white paint on Heidi's rear bumper. Unfortunately, white was the most popular color for Ford F-150s in Brenham. So, the color of the truck was not a tremendous help.

Jon told me, "Detective Larry asked the doctor how long Heidi would be in a coma. The doctor hesitated, looked at me, and said in quiet voice, 'It could be forever.'"

I thought what a blessing it was to have St. Theresa's so close. It would allow Jon and Mertle to visit Heidi even during the harvest activities.

St. Theresa Hospital was started by the Sisters of Selfless Service. They were an order of nuns from Fleetway, Ohio. The original nuns aided travelers as they came through Ohio in the days of the covered wagons. At the turn of the 1900s, they left Fleetway and settled in the Brazos Bottom, and helped the German and Italian settlers settle there. Soon medical services were needed for the new immigrants, so they started providing nursing services and recruited the first doctor to the Bottom. Dr. Fleming was a priest in Fleetway and left the church to become a physician. He was a pious man who treated people for free or for any bartered goods. He would also exchange medical services for chickens and any other livestock. He lived until he was ninety years old. Before he died, he recruited other physicians to care for the farming community of the Brazos Bottom.

Jon had so much on his plate. He needed help. I suggested he may need to call Isabel and Fritz together and set up a meeting.

Jon responded, "I would like to clear the air, and I could use both their support." I told him that I was happy to help as well. We all met. Jon told Fritz he was a vital member of the team.

Fritz said nothing; he just listened. Jon told him that this next harvest day he was to secure the pickers. Isabel and Fritz looked extremely uncomfortable. I wondered if they really did not want to do this. Neither of them seemed overly concerned about Heidi. The rest of us looked at each other with dismay.

After the meeting, Isabel and Fritz went to work. Jon called Martin to ask him to help with the harvest because there was a need. Although he was a bricklayer, building had really slowed down in Brenham. Jon could not reach him. When Jon called Martin's company, they said that he was gone. He had left town on August the seventeenth. No one knew where he went.

Chapter 15

Jon said, "I will ask my wife, Mertle, to join the harvest crew. She used to help me when we first started the vineyard and the winery. She can drive the tractor. She is a teacher, but school is still out for the summer. I know she will be happy to help me."

"See you August twentieth, Jon," I said. I was worried about Fritz getting the pickers, so I called him to see how things were going. Fritz assured me he had it covered.

Luigi and I arrived at the vineyard early to see if we could help. To support the picking and processing, Fritz had to come in early to do the first punch-down of the grape-must. We walked with him into the winery.

When he entered the fermentation room, he stepped back quickly and noted, "The room is full of CO_2." He had to air out the room for 20 minutes. Tank one and tank two were actively fermenting. "Today we will fill tank three," he said. Twelve more tons would be going into tank three.

The pickers arrived. They seemed to know the family and were especially fond of Mertle. Jon looked at her lovingly, put his arm around her, and said, "The pickers love Mertle. If she asked them to stay all night, they would have for her. The pickers are from an orphanage in Cat Springs. They are sixteen- to twenty-year-old students. Many of the orphans had parents who died unexpectedly and there was no family to take care of them. Some children had gotten into trouble. They went into the orphanage instead of juvenile detention. Mertle knew some of them from her teaching job."

"The pickers love being out in the vineyard; they love being among the vines," Jon continued. "They are hired by many vineyards within a 60-mile radius of Cat Springs. We must share the crew with the other vineyards. That is why there are a few days and sometimes a week between harvest days. Mertle and I love working with the orphanage. Their spirit inspires everyone at the winery."

Mertle made cookies and lemonade for each picker. I volunteered to help and asked if she knew Lulu.

"Know Lulu?" Mertle replied. "Of course! She is like part of our family." I was stunned. Neither Heidi nor Lulu had ever mentioned it.

"Lulu was sent to the orphanage here from California. Her family lost their vineyard when her parents were killed in an automobile accident. She was an only child and had no one to care for her. She was transferred to the Brazos Valley Orphanage, where Jon and I helped to care for her."

"She is a very busy girl, but I know she would love to hear from you. Call her now," she said, smiling.

That was uncomfortable, I thought. But I picked up the phone and called the number Heidi had given me. Lulu answered.

"Hi, Lulu. This is Trevor Talan. We met at the Metock harvest." She interrupted, "Hi Trevor, it is so good to hear from you. Have you been practicing the dance steps I taught you?"

I paused, knowing that I hadn't danced since the harvest party, and tried to gather my thoughts. Why was it so hard to talk with this girl?

"I need some more practice," I told her. "Do you want to go to the Texas Hall of Fame?"

"Yes," she exclaimed, "That would be fun. When do you want to go?"

"How about this weekend?" She agreed enthusiastically saying that she would meet me there. I hung up the phone feeling like I was walking ten feet off the ground. Mertle smiled and kept working.

Jon and Fritz processed the grapes, and then Jon told him he could go home. Jon asked him to open the fermentation door before he left.

Expecting Jon home at 10:00 p.m., Mertle said goodbye and told him, "I know it will be a late night tonight. Why don't I just bring you your dinner at 8:00 p.m.?"

She knew that it would be an exceptionally long day and Jon would be very tired. She looked at me and sighed, "I worry that Jon has to climb on top of those tanks when he is already tired, and I am concerned that there may be just too much carbon dioxide and not enough air for Jon to be safe."

I offered to help, but Jon declined, saying that I should go home and get rested for the next day's work. I felt bad leaving, but was relieved to get some rest. It had been a long time since I had done so much physical labor.

The next day Mertle shared, "When I arrived at the winery, Jon was up on top of the tanks punching down. I had to drop off the food outside the room because I could not catch my breath. Jon came out of the room to eat dinner. He was acting giddy, and his speech was slurred. I told him there was too much carbon dioxide."

Jon told me he finished punching down and arrived home at 10:30 p.m. Three tanks were full, two of them were actively fermenting. The next day, Jon asked Fritz to set up the large fan at the door to ventilate the room.

Heidi was still in a coma. Detective Larry had no leads. Heidi's boyfriend was still gone, and no one knew where he was. This was very unusual. Martin often worked out of town, but when he was leaving town, he would tell his friends where he was going. They only had two more harvest days.

The weekend finally came. I was going to see Lulu. Arriving early at the Texas Hall of Fame, I sat at the bar near the door so I could see her when she entered. The rustic look of the ballroom felt so comfortable-like home. The barn-style door opened. A light shining from behind her as she entered the dark bar created a halo around her. I was mesmerized.

She smiled, walked directly to me, extended her hand, and led me to the dance floor. She taught me the Texas Two Step, the waltz, and she even showed me how to line dance. Two hours of dancing made me thirsty. I escorted her to a table for burgers, beer, and the opportunity to sit down. Conversation with her was so easy. It was as though we had known each other for years.

The next harvest day was August the twenty-third. Fritz set it up and everything went well. This time thirty-five pickers came from Cat Springs. Five more pickers had come because the word got out that Mertle was so sweet to them. Lulu and I joined them. This time we finished picking at 2:00 p.m.

Processing went well, and they finished an hour early, which is very unusual. Jon released Fritz to go home and then started the punch downs. The room was full of CO_2. He put the big fan on to vent the room and waited thirty minutes. Jon went into the lab and did all the lab work. The only thing left for him to do was punch down.

Four tanks were filled. Three of them were actively fermenting. After airing the room out for thirty minutes and having the fan exhaust the CO_2, he began doing the punch downs.

Jon was so pleased with the harvest, but he was very concerned about Heidi's health. Everyone was rallying around him and Mertle. Everyone wanted to help. We all thought this could be the best harvest ever. Lulu and I left Jon at the winery and headed to dinner and a little more dancing.

All of the punch downs went extremely well, but Jon did not arrive home until midnight. Mertle could not understand why he came home so late. When Mertle asked where Jon went, Jon said, "I went to see Heidi at the hospital. She recognized me but had no memory of the car accident. She just kept repeating 'bright lights.' Then she would doze in and out of consciousness. She looks like a raccoon! Both eyes are black, and it looks like her head struck the steering wheel as though her car was hit from the rear and her head was thrown back and then whipped forward. The nurse told me that Isabel visited Heidi earlier in the afternoon." Mertle listened quietly with tears in her eyes.

Jon reported, "Heidi is out of the coma, but she is very confused. Detective Larry was there to interview her but was told to come back tomorrow morning. Heidi was in no condition to give a formal statement. I then went to the Big Steer Bar to look for Heidi's boyfriend, Martin. He often went there to get a nightcap before he went home. He wasn't there, and no one knew where he was."

Martin was a regular at the bar, and that concerned Jon.

"When I went to my car, I noticed a Ford F-150 white pickup truck in the back of the parking lot. It was the same type of pickup that I saw in the vineyard. As I walked towards the pickup, it sped off. I became very suspicious." Jon paused as he could see that Mertle was worried.

He put his arms around her and caringly shared, "I took the long way home and went by Heidi's house and Fritz's house. There was a parked car in front of Heidi's house. It obviously was not hers since hers was totaled when she ran off the road. When I passed Fritz's house, his car was gone. I called Detective Larry to let him know."

Mertle told Jon that Isabel had come home right before him. Mertle shook her head, "It is so unusual for Isabel to be out so late, and she went straight to bed. Barely said anything."

Isabel was staying with Jon and Mertle because she became so disturbed after Heidi's car ran off the road.

The last harvest day was August twenty-fourth, the next day. There were so many unanswered questions and loose ends. Detective Larry was frustrated. Heidi almost died. Martin was still missing.

Chapter 16

It was a joyful day. It's always a celebration when the harvest is complete. A two-day celebration ensues. The elders of the church come out to join in the celebration. On the beginning of the last day of harvest, one of the elders led in a prayer:

> *Thank you, Lord, for Your bountiful gift. Thank you to the people who have come to help us with harvest. In Christ's name, Amen.*

On that last day of harvest, forty pickers arrived. They did a fantastic job. After the pick, Mertle brought out boxes of cookies for them to take home as a thank-you gift. Inside each box was also a surprise envelope with bonus cash. Lulu and I each received one as well.

Jon's daughter Isabel worked with us and was so helpful. She knew her dad was very tired, so she offered to do the second punch down that night. Jon at first said no, but he remembered that he had a lot of labs to do. And Isabel had done punch downs previously. He also felt it was her way of reconciling.

Jon told us, "I am planning to take the whole family out for a celebration dinner tonight. You all go home and get ready. Isabell and I will take care of the rest."

Fritz went home. Mertle went to change her clothes and get ready for dinner. Luigi, Lulu, and I left and told Jon we would meet him at the restaurant. Jon went to the lab. Isabel went to the tank room. She opened the door, vented the room, and turned on the fan. Isabel was very meticulous and wanted to make sure that the punch-down was done very safely. Four tanks were actively fermenting, and the fifth tank had just been filled.

I know from experience that the refrigeration tanks run warmer during fermentation. Refrigeration systems often have a hard time keeping up when all of the tanks begin to ferment. The normal temperature for red grape fermentation is 65 degrees F, but the thermometer showed the tanks were at 75 degrees F. It was a very robust fermentation. Isabel would reset the thermostat to try to lower the temperature, but more likely the temperature would stay at 75 degrees F and even go closer to 80 degrees, which is still acceptable.

At 8:00 p.m., Fritz showed up at Jon and Mertle's home to pick up Isabel. No one was there. Fritz went ahead to the restaurant.

Jon came home. Mertle was in the backyard cutting flowers for a table at the restaurant. When Jon asked her about Fritz and Isabel, Mertle said that she had seen Fritz's car drive away and assumed that he and Isabel were already headed to the restaurant. Jon and Mertle went to the restaurant, thinking everyone was waiting for them. Luigi, Lulu, and I arrived at the same time as Jon and Mertle. Isabel was not there.

Everyone looked at Fritz.

Fritz explained, "When I tried to pick up Isabel at the house, no one was there, so I thought everyone had already left to go the restaurant." He looked at Jon and asked if Isabel had left the winery.

Jon stiffened as he said, "I thought Isabel had gone home."

He looked at Mertle, who apologized, saying, "I had been outside and assumed, when I saw Fritz's truck drive away, that he and Isabel had left together."

Jon immediately left the group and called Detective Larry. He informed Detective Larry that Isabel had not shown up at the restaurant or at the house.

He went on to explain, "I was in the lab. Every hour I checked on Isabel. On my first check, I had to turn on the venting fan to higher speed. Isabel had remembered to turn on the fan, but she did not turn it on to the maximum speed. She had already punched down tanks one and two and was working on tank three. When I left, she was punching down tank four. When I returned to the tank room later, Isabel was gone, and I thought Isabel was finished with the punch-down.

"As I entered the room, I heard a loud screech of tires outside as a pickup truck went speeding off. I wondered if Isabel might have been in it. I could not find her, so I assumed that she had finished the punch-down of the final tank and had gone home."

Detective Larry listened and then responded that he had interviewed Heidi that morning and said he wanted to speak to the family. He said he had interesting news from Heidi that he wanted to give to them face to face.

Jon understood but was emphatic, "Yes, I want to know, but right now I want you to find Isabel. I do not know where she is. There was no friction today. I was very pleased with Isabel. She had volunteered to punch-down four tanks. I told her how proud I was when I saw her in the tank room. Now

I am concerned about that speeding pickup that left the winery property."

Detective Larry said he would send out a detail to search for her. The next morning at the Metock's home, Larry reported, "Heidi did not see the face of the person who ran her off the road, but the car was white, and it was a Ford F-150. She said the pickup pushed the back of her car, causing hers to spin out of control and run into the ditch, striking the tree. She told me the driver had to know how to do that so must have had some previous training."

Detective Larry said he asked Heidi if she knew where Martin was. "Heidi did not know where he was and acted surprised that Martin hadn't been to see her while she was in the hospital."

He asked Jon, "How did Heidi and Martin meet?"

Jon replied, "Heidi and Martin met at Mertle and my twentieth wedding anniversary party at Villari Italian Restaurant in Brenham. Martin had done some bricklaying work for me when we added onto our home. It was a wonderful dinner of veal parmesan. The wine was very special to us. It was a Messina Hof Sagrantino. We are very fond of Sagrantino and decided to plant it in our vineyard as well.

"Martin was seated next to Heidi. They really hit it off. They started dating right after the anniversary party. It looked like the relationship could be serious. Heidi liked Martin because he drove a fast sports car and had a motorcycle. He is very mechanical and fixes all of his vehicles himself. Outwardly he was a model citizen, but some suspected he appeared to be too good.”

Jon continued, “Before the accident, Heidi said that Martin had been acting very strangely, and she was concerned about his lack of work. She said that Martin was becoming desperate for money.

“Heidi confessed to me that she had been seeing other men. Because their relationship was stressful, Heidi had started dating again. Martin was drinking more, and his personality was becoming more aggressive and more impulsive; his wild side was showing more and more. Heidi was no longer thinking of Martin as a potential husband.”

Detective Larry reported that Heidi revealed that the new man in her life was Sammy D. Detective Larry asked the Metocks if they knew Sammy D. Both Jon and Mertle looked surprised.

Detective Larry shared, “Sammy D. is in life insurance and had convinced Heidi to take out a large life insurance policy. He is a short, stocky, charming, and good-looking man with black hair that was slicked back like it was plastered to his head. He wears very bright clothes and is reputed to own fifty pairs of shoes. Heidi shared that they met at his big Valentine’s Day party he throws for his customers. She was intrigued by his Chicago accent.

“When I questioned her about the insurance policy beneficiary, Heidi became defensive of Sammy D., saying, ‘I made Isabel the beneficiary of my life insurance policy. Even though we did not always get along and yes, sometimes we hated each other, the special bond between twins goes very deep.'

"Sammy D. and I had three or four dates, and I thought it could get serious. Martin and I had been together a long time, but it never seemed like it was going to result in marriage."

Detective Larry shared that Fritz told him Heidi had also been dating his older brother, Hans. Hans was a big pot-bellied Brenham police officer who was very persistent in his pursuit of Heidi. When Detective Larry mentioned Hans, Heidi admitted, "I did date him for a while, but he seemed too aggressive, and we just fought all the time."

She continued. "Hans caught Martin speeding in his sports car. Martin told Hans that he was not speeding. The two of them had words, and Hans wrote him up for battery of a police officer after Martin pushed him. Martin received a $1,000 fine and was put on six months' probation. Martin swore he would get even with Hans.

"Hans was a Brenham High School football star. He played on the state championship team and was one of the team captains. He played tackle and even got a scholarship to play for State University. Hans loved working out in the gym and could leg press and bench-press more than any other lineman. Even though he was a freshman, he started on the varsity team. He had long blond hair and was extremely popular with the ladies. I was even smitten with him and admired his athletic ability. In the last game of his freshman year, he had a horrible knee injury while playing against State's chief rival, Lone Star.

"He was knocked out on the field, and some thought he was dead. Then suddenly someone from the sidelines ran out onto the field. He jumped on Hans and resuscitated him. It was a miracle."

Luigi and I looked at each other. In unison we shouted, "It was Bubba!" Heidi looked at us like we were possessed and asked, "How did you know?" Luigi shared his story and we all agreed that that moment that Bubba felt driven to run to the field had to be God inspired.

Heidi went on, "When Hans hurt his knee, his football career and his scholarship were lost. He went into a deep depression, his grades fell, and he dropped out of State. His whole personality was rooted in his football persona. When football was gone, he could not relate to people. He dropped out of life. He left town and moved to east Texas, where he worked at a crawfish farm. After three seasons, Hans seemed to find himself. He had gained fifty pounds and lost his hair. He applied to the County Sheriff's Department and enrolled in the Brazos Bottom Junior College to study law enforcement. It gave him a new spirit to get in shape.

"The Sergeant was a fan of Hans when he played in high school, so he gave him a job. I started dating him shortly after he joined the County Sheriff's Department. I was proud of him and his determination to come back."

Chapter 17

Detective Larry then turned his attention towards Isabel. There was still no word from her. She never showed up at home or at the restaurant. Detective Larry wanted to go to the winery and check it out. Jon and Larry arrived at the winery and unlocked the fermentation door. As the door opened, the rush of CO_2 gas escaped the room. They turned on the light and turned on the fan to maximum speed. Detective Larry said there was no way a person could breathe in that room.

Jon assured Detective Larry that before working in the room, Isabel had completely vented the room and that was normal procedure. The fan blew out much of the CO_2, and the open door allowed oxygen to refill the room. There was a large candle in the room that was lit when they first entered the room. At first the candle would not light, but as the oxygen entered the room, the candle would light. If the candle stayed lit, that meant that there was sufficient oxygen to work in the room.

Detective Larry asked Jon to show him how the punch-down was done. They both climbed up the ladder and stood on the two-inch by ten-inch planks and started punching down tank one, then tank two, then tank three, then tank four, and then tank five. When they started punching down tank five, the tank that Isabel would have done last, a scarf came to the surface of the grape skins. Detective Larry told Jon not to touch anything. They put on latex gloves. Larry pulled the scarf out of the tank and carefully examined it.

Suddenly a human hand reached out through the grape skins. Jon almost passed out. He fell to his knees, grabbed the hand, and started to pull. There on the hand was the ring that he had given Isabel the year before. It symbolized his commitment to Isabel that she would take over the winery. His heart sank. Larry and Jon lifted Isabel's lifeless body out of the tank. Jon burst into tears. Isabel was his favorite daughter and the heir apparent to his winery dynasty. There was dark red wine everywhere. Isabel was covered in wine. It looked like she was drenched in blood. They carefully carried her body down the ladder and placed her on the floor.

Detective Larry said, "It looks like Isabel fell into the wine tank. Or was she pushed?" He called the coroner to arrange for her transfer and to investigate the site. Jon just stared at the floor as he clung to Isabel's hand. Larry suggested he go home to Mertle. Jon slowly walked to the house to tell his wife the horrific news. Jon kept asking "God, why? Why? Why?" He had been so protective of Isabel, and telling his wife this news was the hardest thing he had ever had to do in his life. Jon knew how much Mertle loved her children and that she would be devastated. He also knew that Mertle felt that Isabel was the perfect one to take over the winery.

As Jon was walking toward the house, he ran into Fritz, who was cleaning the crush pad. Jon told Fritz the shocking news about Isabel. Fritz began to cry. Profound grief quickly moved to anger as he stared at Jon. "I am not surprised. You should never have asked her to do punch-downs anyway."

Fritz sorrowfully mumbled, "I should have been the one doing the punch-downs." Jon was very surprised with Fritz's response. Jon was the only one who knew that he had asked Isabel to do the punch-downs. How did Fritz know?

He set that thought aside to focus on Mertle. Once he reached the house, he asked Mertle to please sit down because he had terrible news to share with her. Jon sat by her and held her hand while he relayed the story of Isabel's death. Mertle squeezed his hand and closed her eyes as large tears streamed down her cheeks. She bowed her head as if to pray. Jon cradled her in his arms and rocked her back and forth while he, too, cried. Mertle wanted to see her Isabel. Jon walked arm in arm with Mertle to the winery. There they saw her lifeless body. She looked like she was asleep. Unfortunately, Isabel would not awaken from this sleep.

Chapter 18

The coroner, Dr. Gretel, had arrived and inspected the scene. He and his team were ready to move her body to his laboratory. Mertle knelt by her daughter's body and spoke through tears, "Isabel, I love you so much. You have always been the rock of our family. You tried so hard. I am so thankful for you and proud of you. We will miss you so much!" Her voice broke between tears and gasps of breath. Finally, she said goodbye. Jon knelt with Mertle in silence, holding her close to him.

The coroner's team took Isabel's body away to his laboratory in the basement of the old Brenham Hospital. Dr. Gretel had been the coroner in the Bottom for more than thirty years. I learned that he was trained in Arkansas and left Little Rock after a suspicious time as a surgeon at Little Rock General. Jon told me, "The rumor was that Dr. Gretel performed a bowel resection and the patient died. When they performed the autopsy, the pathologist discovered a scalpel blade left in the resected bowel. As the patient began walking, the blade severed the bowel and the patient bled out. Fortunately for Dr. Gretel, the patient was eighty-nine years old and had no family to sue Dr. Gretel.

"Dr. Gretel moved here from Little Rock and has been the coroner here ever since. Now all of Dr. Gretel's patients are dead on arrival. He is a likeable man who never married and lives alone. He doesn't socialize with anyone in the community, but he has a strange hobby collecting butterflies. He is said to have the largest dead-butterfly collection in Texas."

Detective Larry started interviewing Fritz. Fritz said Jon sent him home right after they finished crushing the grapes. "I even left the crush pad without cleaning it. I didn't know that Jon asked Isabel to do the punch-downs. I would have stayed to help her." Fritz continued, "I came in early the next morning to finish cleaning up. Still, I had not heard from Isabel. It was not like her to not respond." A tear came to Fritz's eye.

Detective Larry asked Fritz if Isabel had any enemies. Fritz told him, "Isabel and Heidi did not get along. They were both expecting to take over the winery. They both knew that only one of them would win. The favor of Jon and Mertle was critical to both girls. Jon gave that ring to Isabel to show his favor for her, but then he began to rely on Heidi for everything."

The next day Detective Larry went to see Dr. Gretel at the coroner's office. Dr. Gretel said Isabel had died of carbon dioxide poisoning, but when he examined her more closely, he found that she had been with a man before she died. Dr. Gretel asked Larry, "So, was this a sex crime?"

Detective Larry went back to Jon and asked, "Did Isabel have a boyfriend?

Jon said, "She and Fritz had started a relationship, but it was called off." Larry told Jon that Isabel had had been with a man before she died. Jon exploded and called out to God to save Isabel's soul. His anguish turned to anger, and he ran out shouting that he was going to kill Fritz. Larry ran after Jon, fearing that he might really kill Fritz. As Jon confronted

Fritz and told him the coroner's findings, Larry stood between them.

Fritz was obviously shaken. He told Jon, "I loved Isabel, and our relationship was never called off. We had been seeing each other secretly in the vineyard. Isabel told me that you had seen a white truck in the vineyard. That truck belonged to me. We were planning to get married despite your objections. We had planned to tell you and Mertle at the dinner. Isabel knew the dinner was a celebration and joyous occasion for everyone and hoped that you would agree to our marriage. I did go back to the tank room where Isabel was doing punch-downs, and we made love in the tank room."

He went on to say, "When I left Isabel, she was alive and getting ready to punch-down tank five. I offered to do it, but she wanted to be able to tell you that she did all the work. She wanted to gain your favor before you announced who was going to take over the winery. She even put together her own wine blends and submitted them into a competition, hoping for a medal to prove her worth to the winery. I shipped them for her myself.

"Isabel also thought that by performing all of the duties that you wanted her to do, when she and I announced our marriage, you would be more inclined to give us your blessing." Fritz said that when he was leaving the tank room, he could hear Jon coming from the lab, so he jumped in his pickup truck and sped off. Jon realized the sound of the pickup truck leaving the winery was Fritz's pickup truck. When Jon entered the room and saw Isabel on the top of tank five, he knew that when Fritz had left the property, Isabel was alone and alive.

Jon reflected, "Isabel did seem happy that night when I last saw her, and her spirits were very expressive, more than usual. I remember it gave me a sense of comfort and confidence that I could return to the lab because Isabel seemed to have everything under control and was doing such a good job with the punch-downs. But when I went back to the fermentation room an hour later, I didn't see Isabel; but I just thought that she finished and went home."

Detective Larry now had to solve a suspected murder. "Isabel had done the punch downs to four tanks without an incident. The fermentation room was completely aired out, so it looks like she did not pass out and fall into the tank. It looks like someone may have pushed Isabel into the tank and then left the light on."

Next, Detective Larry had to figure out who hated Isabel enough to do this. He had the body of Isabel and a scarf that looked like a headband. Larry asked Jon if he had ever seen Isabel wear a headband scarf.

Jon said, "Isabel hated hats and never wore a headband." Detective Larry asked Fritz if Isabel was wearing a scarf headband the night they made love in the tank room. Fritz said no. This scarf was a smoking gun for the detective. He sent it to Houston for DNA detection, but was concerned that the grape-must might have erased all the DNA and that it took weeks to get results.

Chapter 19

Detective Larry turned his attention to Heidi's car accident. He looked at the police report and realized the investigating officer was Hans. Hans had dated Heidi. Detective Larry spoke with Officer Hans, who said, "When I arrived at the scene, Heidi was unconscious, and her car was stopped by a tree. I immediately called for an ambulance and wrote it up. It appeared that she had lost control of the car and had run off the road." Detective Larry noted that the report was unusually brief, which made it very suspicious. It was not like Officer Hans's normal investigations.

That afternoon when Larry returned to the police station, he saw that officer Han's front bumper had a dent on it. When Larry examined Heidi's car, her right back bumper had a dent. Detective Larry took trace samples of Officer Hans' bumper and found that the paint had a perfect match to Heidi's rear bumper. That night, Detective Larry called Officer Hans into his office. "Officer Hans," Larry began, "can you please explain why the paint on your damaged vehicle bumper is a match to the paint on Heidi Metock's vehicle bumper?"

Officer Hans admitted, "I was driving my personal vehicle on my way to work. It's a white Ford F-150 pickup truck. When I saw Heidi's car, I sped up to talk with her. She suddenly put on her brakes. I tried to avoid her car as I swerved to the right, but I hit her right rear bumper. She spun out of control, sir. She didn't look as though she would have been hurt because she hit the tree at an extremely low speed.

"I was so embarrassed by the accident that I left the scene and started my shift. But then my conscience began to bother me. I returned to the scene, expecting that she would have a wrecker there and that she was on her way home. It was such a small accident. But when I arrived, I was shocked to see that Heidi was still unconscious. I was unaware that Heidi did not have her seatbelt on and that the minor accident was worse than I had thought. Her head had struck the windshield.

"I realized that I was guilty of leaving the scene of an accident and called the ambulance so as not to be suspected."

Detective Larry felt that Heidi's mystery was solved. He knew that Hans had shown extremely poor judgement and would spend time in jail, but Isabel was still a puzzle to solve. Who killed Isabel, and who owned the scarf? Who wanted Isabel dead? He knew it was not Fritz. Jon had heard him drive off. It could not have been Heidi, because she was in no shape to do it, even though she had motive.

The DNA report came in. It revealed that the scarf belonged to a male. The male's DNA was not in the police system, so Detective Larry needed to get DNA samples of all the males in her life. He obtained a warrant and was able to obtain DNA samples from all males at the winery and all males who were associated with Isabel. He then turned his attention to the males who knew Heidi. Maybe it was one of Heidi's boyfriends?

Hans had left the scene of the accident, but was incapable of murder. Or was he? He said he never wore a headband.

Detective Larry secured a DNA sample from Hans. The report was inconclusive.

Next, Larry brought in Sammy D. Larry had done some research on Sammy's past and found that he had been from Chicago and his father was in jail for murder. His mother was born in Palermo. Her father, Tino, was born in Poggiali, a small town outside of Palermo. They had an arranged marriage. Tino got in trouble with the local police after he was accused of killing a local politician. The police could not prove that Tino was the killer. Tino moved to Chicago and got into the garbage collection business.

Sammy was a troubled youth. He joined a gang at a very young age and got his GED because he was such a poor student. He admitted that he had moved to Brenham twelve months ago because his father was in prison for murder. He needed a fresh start. His uncle Tony Joe had lived in Brenham for more than ten years, was a respected businessman, and helped Sammy open his insurance agency, which now insures most of the Brazos Bottom Wine families.

He gave a DNA sample, freely. He had only met Isabel once and thought she was a wonderful young lady. His DNA report came back, and Sammy D. was cleared.

Detective Larry's attention turned to Heidi's long-term boyfriend, Martin. Martin had supposedly been out of town, and no one knew where he was. Larry asked some of Martin's friends. They said he had returned to town a few days ago. That was new information. Detective Larry checked the local bars and motorcycle tracks and found Martin. Larry took him in for interrogation.

Martin claimed that he was staying out of town. Larry asked where he was. Martin said that he had taken a job as a bricklayer in a new subdivision called Harvest Green in Richmond, Texas. When Detective Larry began to interview Martin, he began sweating profusely, and his glasses were fogged up. He had a bald head and sweat poured down his face. He was wearing a brand-new yellow headband.

Martin said," No one knew where I was because I got a call at 5:00 p.m. and was told to report to the job site the next morning at 7:00 a.m. The company put me up at the Best Western off of the Katy Freeway." Martin said Detective Larry could check with the motel and check out his story. Larry followed up and found that Martin checked out of the motel the day of Isabel's alleged murder.

Detective Larry went back to Martin's job site. Martin had left at 1:00 p.m. that afternoon because he claimed he was too hot. Detective Larry went to Martin's apartment and saw him packing up to leave town. Detective Larry took Martin down to the police station for suspicion of murder and was able to obtain a DNA sample and detained him overnight in the jail. When the DNA report came in, it was a perfect match to the headband scarf that they found in the tank with Isabel's body.

Martin claimed that Isabel loved his headbands and would wear them when they were together. Martin also said that he and Isabel were secretly in love and that she was going to leave town with Martin after harvest. That is why he was packing.

Chapter 20

Detective Larry told him the results and asked, "What was the motive?" Martin put his head in his hands and said, "When I arrived back in town from Houston and found that Heidi's car was forced off the road, I just knew it had to be Isabel. They were always arguing. So, I went to the winery and saw Fritz coming out of the tank room. I hid until he left and then looked all over the winery for Isabel. The lights were off except in the tank room where the fermentation was occurring. I went into the room and saw Isabel standing on the wooden plank punching down the must. I accused Isabel of pushing Heidi's car off the road. She said she wished she had, but she didn't.

"Then she told me, 'While you were out of town, Martin, Heidi was dating all these new guys and told me that you were on the way out. Heidi said that she was going to dump you.'" Martin was enraged. Isabel even told Martin that Heidi had fallen in love with Sammy D. She said, "The two of them drink together at the bar. And he drives a 1957 red Thunderbird."

Martin clinched his fists, stood up and angrily spewed, "I could not believe what I was being told, and I just blew up. I started climbing up the ladder. As I climbed up the ladder, I bumped my head on the wooden planks. I guess my headband flew off into the tank."

Detective Larry took it from there, "When your head hit the wooden plank, it made Isabel unstable, and she fell into the tank."

Martin said, "I immediately finished the climb to the top of the tank and tried to grab her. I reached toward her with the push-down tool and wanted to save her. I did not mean to hurt her! But it was too late. Isabel had sunk into the grape-must. I threw the punch-down tool down to the ground and put my hand into the must to try to grab her arm, but her arm was gone. Isabel was gone."

Martin panicked, "I knew I had to get out of there as soon as I could. Plus, I was not used to being in that low-oxygen environment and started feeling like I was going to pass out. So, I quickly slid down the ladder and ran out of the room."

Detective Larry added, "You left all the lights on, closed the door, and quietly walked to the parking lot and drove off. You told yourself it was a complete accident and that you had no intention of hurting Isabel. You were angry. You were enraged, but you were not interested in killing Isabel. She was just the messenger."

Martin never reported it. And he never told anyone what he had done. But now the truth had come out. Detective Larry told him that he was going to pursue murder charges. Martin kept pleading with Detective Larry, telling him it was an accident. He had no intention of hurting her.

Martin knew that a long trial in town would devastate everyone. Detective Larry told him that if he pleaded guilty to involuntary manslaughter, Detective Larry would talk with the District Attorney to give him leniency. Detective Larry began to explain to Martin, "If you do not plead guilty, you will be charged with first degree murder and will get life in prison. There will be a trial, and the whole town will be talking."

Martin was from a longtime Brenham family. His father had served as mayor and his mom was the school principal. Martin was proud of his dad, Kuno, for winning a very hard-fought race for mayor against Heidi's dad, Jon, who had been mayor for two terms.

Detective Larry continued, "Kuno is extremely popular with the cotton farmers and highly supported by the police. He is a real law-and-order man. Once he caught a man stealing brick and stone from one of his jobs. He ran after the culprit and subdued him, tied him up, and took him to the police station all by himself. The newspaper published a big story about the arrest just before the election, so Kuno was a hero and the new mayor."

Martin was afraid this would ruin his family in Brenham. He kept repeating it was an accident. Detective Larry then told Martin that if he pleaded guilty to involuntary manslaughter, there would be less of an impact on his family. Martin could tell the newspaper it was an accident. Martin could say he never meant to hurt Isabel.

The town of Brenham was buzzing with the news. Officer Hans was fired from the police force and then was charged with a third-degree felony and had to spend one year in jail. The judge suspended his jail time, and he was put on three years' probation. Officer Hans left town in disgrace, and no one heard from him again.

Martin pleaded guilty to involuntary manslaughter and was sentenced to ten years. He served out his sentence in

Huntsville prison, and Heidi visited him occasionally. Heidi took over running the winery and got engaged to Sammy D. After Martin went to jail, Heidi and Sammy D. became close. Heidi loved the way he fussed over her. He was good-looking, financially successful, and respectful of Jon and Mertle. They both like Sammy D. a lot. He would even help Heidi with her winery duties. Both Jon and Mertle hoped that Heidi and Sammy D. would marry and be able to work together at the winery.

Fritz missed Isabel tremendously. He could not stay in Brenham after Isabel died. There was nothing holding him here. He moved to work at a winery in California. He met Don Brady in Paso Robles. He applied to Don as a cellar hand and went out to Paso Robles to interview. Don took a liking to Fritz. When he interviewed, Fritz impressed Don with his diversified experience. He could work the crush pad and work the barrels. Fritz received the word that Don wanted him to join his winery. Fritz packed up his things and moved to Paso Robles.

Detective Larry was offered a promotion. Luigi stayed at the *Brenham Daily News* and became the editor when Bubba Biggie retired. I completed my assignment of writing the Texas wine history of the Brazos Bottom for Buddy Hagner of the Knights of the Vine with even more personal details of the people behind the wines.

Chapter 21

The murder on the Brazos taught me many things. Families need to love and not hate. Hatred only brings pain. Heidi spent the rest of her life regretting the bad feelings that existed between her and Isabel.

Hans learned that it is better to face up to what you have done than try to hide your actions. It only leads to more dire punishment.

Martin learned to control his rage and anger. His anger had resulted in the death of a good person.

Heidi ran the winery.

Jon and Mertle began traveling. Before they left for their first trip, they attended the awards banquet for the Best of the Bottom Wine Competition. Five hundred attended, and the governor was there to make the presentation. Heidi and Sammy D. were there. Detective Larry and his wife, Ann, were there. Grape grower Charlie and Maria Gee were there. And they graciously invited me to sit at their table. I invited Lulu. I think she may be the one. One chair was left empty in honor of Isabel.

The governor spoke about the importance of agriculture and the Brazos Bottom to the State of Texas. He acknowledged the problems of dicamba overdrift and thanked the growers for pursuing truth and bringing a light to the issue. He then presented the awards.

"The Top White Wine award, which is a Blanc du Bois, goes to Nider Winery. It scored a perfect 100. Congratulations!" he cheered. The audience clapped enthusiastically.

"The Top Red Wine award, which is a naturally fermented Port Wine made from the Lenoir grape, goes to Metock Winery. It scored a perfect 100." Everyone began to cheer. The governor raised his hands and said, "Wait, there is more."

He continued, "The Best Overall Winery award goes to the winery that achieved the highest average score for all wines submitted. This honor goes to Metock Winery! Congratulations!" The audience was on its feet.

Jon and Mertle looked at the empty chair and slowly walked hand in hand to the podium to receive the award. Jon took the microphone, "On behalf of Mertle, me, our family, and winery team, we thank you all—the judges, our friends and neighbors who have stood by us and supported us always, and most of all to our precious Isabel who was the winemaker for these wines. She had the kindest heart and loved her family. She was a great winemaker who died too soon. Her creativity, vision for the future, and groundbreaking sequential inoculation set her apart in the wine world."

Imagine making a Port wine without the addition of Brandy. The Portuguese have been making Port wines by adding distilled spirits for centuries. When Isabel began using sequential inoculation, everyone in the Brazos Bottom was skeptical. She was convinced it would work. She convinced her father to try. He agreed.

"Now Isabel is gone, but her spirit and innovation will live on at Metock Winery."

Families of the Brazos Bottom

Galle

The Galle family was from Palermo, Sicily. They were a dark and secretive group that kept to themselves, but always had many people around them at their home which locals called the "Compound." There were rumors that they had mafia connections.

Alfonse and Ester Galle had four children – Peter, Tony, Violet, and Rose. Peter was the winemaker and Tony ran the bottling line. Rose and Violet worked at the thirty-acre vineyard. Rose attended UC Davis in California to study viticulture. She was good at math, maintaining equipment and understood the science of growing grapes, but was not good at driving. In fact, Violet was always fearful when Rose got on the tractor.

Violet was good at running equipment but terrible at math, so Rose had to manage the calculations of what to spray and how to mix it. Violet would do the spraying.

On a personal note, the sons caused the parents some grief. Peter hosted gambling parties in his home and bet on horse races in Kentucky. Both boys had reputations for gambling and drinking. The girls were sweet and very dedicated to their family but fearful of their father.

Metock family

Jon and Mertle Metock came to the Brazos Bottom from Bingen, Germany, which was along the Rhine. They have two daughters – fraternal twins, Heidi and Isabel.

Heidi is a small girl with jet black hair and a reputation as an extrovert wild-child that hates school. Introverted Isabel is tall, blond, straight-A student who is very respectful, but is self-conscious due to her exaggerated limp when she walks. Both girls work in the winery with their father.

Known as a hard-working Lutheran Confession family, red-headed Jon's word is his bond and contracts are by handshake. He is a dedicated husband and father and works diligently to be a peacemaker among the five families. Precision in all things is important to him.

Mertle loves to cook and acts as mom to all. She is a schoolteacher who also has worked shoulder to shoulder with Jon. She even drives the tractor.

Nider family

Alder Nider was a chocolatier who came to Brenham after World War I from Koblenz, Germany in the Rhine Valley. Alder considered himself a Prussian and had refused the draft in Germany. He opened a bakery in Brenham.

Alder's grandson Bob and wife, Dolphie, had two daughters – Annie and Beulah. Bob studied winemaking at U.C. Davis and is known as one of Texas' finest winemakers. He is precise and demanding.

Dolphie learned the tradition of chocolate making from Alder and continued the tradition in the bakery with the help of her two daughters.

Beulah manages the catering for the bakery as well as works in the vineyard. She married Presley, who takes care of the equipment at the winery. They had three children – Frans, Frasie, and Flor.

Flirtatious Annie also works in the vineyard and married Blue, who oversees the bottling line, and they had two children – Flory and Martin.

The entire family worked in the winery and vineyard to help Bob.

Bonder family

Greg Bonder managed the BonderKisty winery and Bonder vineyards. He is a private but pragmatic businessman who believes in attacking problems head on. A sense of "I am in control" exudes from him. At any meeting, he rises as the leader.

Kisty family

Phillip Kisty's oldest son Ben was a strapping, God-fearing man who married a Bonder daughter, creating the BonderKisty Winery. Ben's brother, Louis, worked at the winery and oversaw construction projects. The BonderKisty winery was the largest in the region.

Louis had a quick temper and possessive personality.

Gee family

Charlie Gee came to the Brazos Bottom from Napa, California. Charlie developed and managed vineyards there for twenty years. Maria Gee immigrated to the Brazos Bottom with her family from Monterrey, Mexico, to escape the cartel. They met at a harvest festival in Napa, married, and moved to the Brazos Bottom.

Charlie opened his Charlie Gee Vineyard Consulting business in Brenham and had planted a vineyard on Maria's family land.

Jeffries family

Bill and Fatama Jeffries came from Winnie, Texas. Bill was a military policeman who had met his wife overseas when he was serving in the military in Iraq as an interrogator. After leaving the military, he continued in law enforcement and in keeping his marine type of physique. Fatama was quiet, but always helping those around her.

About the Authors

Paul V. and Merrill Bonarrigo founded Messina Hof Vineyard in 1977 in Bryan, Texas, as pioneers of the Texas grape and wine industries. Today, Messina Hof has four wineries around Texas and continues to be one of the most awarded wineries in Texas in regional, national, and international competitions. The Messina Hof legacy continues with their son, Paul, and his wife, Karen.

Paul V. Bonarrigo, born in the shadow of Yankee Stadium and graduated from Columbia University, served in the Navy during Vietnam and studied winemaking at the University of California–Davis while stationed in California. Merrill Bonarrigo, a native of Bryan–College Station, Texas, graduated from Texas A&M University with a degree in business management and taught Wine Retailing at University of Houston.

Paul and Merrill introduced Sagrantino grapes to Texas. They have traveled to thirty-eight countries to teach wine hospitality and successful generational transition. They lead wine tour groups around the world, blog, and write books:

Ultimate Food and Wine Pairing Cookbook

Ultimate Food and Wine Pairing Cookbook II

Vineyard Cuisine, Meals, and Memories from Messina Hof

Family, Tradition and Romance—The Messina Hof Story

Curse of Estacado—The Trail of Blood and Wine